Praise for JILL

"Fabulously **CREATIVE!** in characterization and setting moods. Her stories read like some of the ancient myths, like CuChullain and other Scottish Celtic tales." Roberto Rodriguez, Webmaster, Strongblade.com

"Svoboda is truly a **WONDERFUL** writer. I find laughs and tears in all her stories." Robert Feher, philosopher

"**BEAUTIFUL** portrayals and story lines. Reminds me of Ursula LeGuin." Kimberly Hines, medical writer and editor

"**ENCHANTING!** I love the mystical elements." Ida Sorci, medical librarian

"Eminently **READABLE.** "Svoboda's stories move seamlessly from topic to event. She makes the writing look so easy." Wayne Allen Sallee, author of The Holy Terror and several other novels and collections, five-time Stoker Award finalist (first novel, collection, novella, novelette, short story); 10 appearances in DAW's Year's Best Horror stories and more.

Sign of the Black Horse & Other Stories

By
Jill Vogel Svoboda

First Paper Book Printing May, 2016
Cover and book design by Johanna M Bolton

This book is available from Amazon in both paper and
eBook format. It also may be purchased from
IDBPI@gmail.com.
For additional information, visit our Web site at
www.idbpi.wordpress.com

IDBPI & the Digital Book logo are trademarks belonging to the
International Digital Book Publishing Industries.

PRINTED IN THE
UNITED STATES OF AMERICA

First Edition

WCD 10 9 8 7 6 5 4 3 2 1

DEDICATION

To my ever-patient &
encouraging husband,
Al Svoboda

Contents

LOVE AND LOVERS

LOVE IS PLEASIN' — SOMETIMES

IT'S A HARD LIFE

HEROES AND VILLAINS

BIRDS AND BEASTS

FANTASTIC WORLDS

HARD TRAVELIN'

love & lovers

And ruin'd love, when it is built anew
grows fairer than at first, more strong,
far greater.

— William Shakespeare, Sonnet 119

A Good Offense

Winter. Florida. The words refuse to be juxta-posed. They repel each other like a pair of magnetic Scottie dogs placed positive pole to positive pole. Antitheses. Antagonists. Nouns in a state of eternal enmity, dueling like Montagues and Capulets.

Sometimes, like Romeo and Juliet, Winter and Florida sneak around, holding hands along the rivers, embracing each other atop the sand hills, and even kissing in the orange groves, to the great distress of the orange growers.

Or they may face off like boxers in the ring. In one corner stands Winter, a Swede, probably, with

blond hair sheared short, like snow that's been lev-
eled by a snow blower, and eyes blue as Lake Erie
ice. He's tall, thin, hard, strong. Well, perhaps not so
thin anymore, and more gray than blond. But he's
strong still.

In the opposite corner preens Florida. She's a
curvaceous brunette, an Italian or perhaps a Cuban,
with thick, wavy hair and brown eyes flecked with
green. Maybe she's more plump than curvy now,
and the smile lines around her mouth cut deep, but
she's still a looker.

Poised in the center of the ring: Mother Nature.
The referee for this duel, she will attempt to ensure
that the opponents play by the rules. Can she pre-
vent the catastrophe that will ensue if Winter and
Florida come to blows? Forgetting for a moment that
an audience is watching, she wrings her hands nerv-
ously.

The starting bell sounds, sending a flock of startled cattle egrets flurrying into the air.

It's December. Winter's heralds roll down the
interstates that link New England, New York, New
Jersey, Pennsylvania, Ohio, Michigan and Indiana to
the Sunshine State. Snowbirds, mutters Florida,
shuddering in distaste and fear as she watches the
newcomers cross over the Georgia border, driving
enormous buses fitted out with beds and stoves, re-
frigerators and showers. Aboard these vehicles ride
refugees from the frigid north, along with cup-
boards full of wool sweaters shed somewhere south
of Knoxville and dresser drawers packed with hal-
ters and shorts for the tropical warmth they expect
once they reach the great sandbar that is Florida.

But wait. Has not Winter already preceded them? The Florida hickories and sweet gums have shed their leaves, and the pastures have faded to brown. What says the thermometer in the morning mist? Fifty degrees? No, forty? No, thirty-seven? The dawn frost shimmers on the sere brown grass.

The battle is not so easily lost. By noon, Florida reasserts herself. At the RV parks, the snowbirds don bathing suits and douse themselves with sunblock. Toledo was never like this, muses Carl Swenson as he steers his Mini Winnie down I-75. He bought the RV used, not so old really, just a few years, and it handles well enough considering its size, he guesses. He's used to driving the Ford Focus that's hitched to Winnie's rear, the "towed" or "toad" in the RV parlance he's been learning as he's worked his way from campground to campground.

Carl has no definite plans. He retired in July, one day after his sixty-second birthday, one year too late for Janice, his wife of thirty-seven years and the mother of their two sons, who are now married with children of their own. His daily golf games with the geezers at the Heather Downs Country Club had worn thin by September. As October approached, he decided he'd like to travel awhile, to explore, and mostly to escape winter's cold rains and freezing snows. Hence the Mini Winnie, his ticket to a balmy new world he has never visited.

Like Carl, the Winnie is of an age that requires some patching. A thunderstorm south of Macon had revealed two leaky windows, one bad enough that at first he thought that Chester, his golden Lab, had piddled on the floor. But when Chester demanded his afternoon walk, Carl had to conclude that the dog wasn't the problem. So today he is looking for a Wal-Mart where he can buy some caulk. Still none too experienced at driving the Winnie, Carl's looking for a Supercenter with a parking lot big enough to pull the RV in and out again without having to back up.

Carl is nearing Florida exit 314 when he spots a Wal-Mart just east of the interstate. He steers carefully down the exit ramp and turns left toward the store. Then a right turn, and he's in the lot, which is almost full. License plates everywhere proclaim that he's not the only snowbird–he sees Michigan, New York, New Jersey, Massachusetts, Wisconsin, even Ontario–but nary a Florida tag in sight. That's fine with Carl. He can talk to northerners. He's a little bit shy of the natives, even though he hasn't yet met any. It occurs to him to wonder if natives actually exist.

Where can Carl park his rig and his toad? There ought to be a section somewhere off to the side where the big RVs go. This lot is certainly full of them, one monster after another, diagonally aligned in the big spots, ready to pull straight out. No room for him, though. All he wants is a tube of caulk, for Chrissake. He doesn't want to wait for someone with a big rig to emerge from the store and pull out. In the end he parks in one of the regular lanes, taking up two whole spaces. The toad sticks out a little too far. So what? He'll be on the road again in a few moments. But then his perfectionist Swedish conscience pricks him: If you can't do it right, don't do it at all.

He starts the engine again. The toad is off on an angle, so he'll need to pull forward, straighten it out, back up again. Concentrating on the view in his mirror, he is startled by a metallic clang in the vicinity of Winnie's front end. He backs up, pulls forward again, the significance of the clang not registering. The sound repeats, accompanied this time by a loud, feminine scream. Carl sticks his head out the side window, looking for the scream's source. He sees the demure nose of a mauve Lincoln Town Car. The rest of the car is–oh, no, the Winnie's nose is poking into the passenger side. Carl backs up, turns off his ignition and gets out to assess the damage.

The Lincoln's driver, a woman, is staring at the huge dent. Both doors are crumpled. Carl can tell just by looking at them that neither door will function. He realizes unhappily that he's through traveling for the day. What to do? He thinks out loud, muttering under his breath: Exchange driver's licenses. Produce insurance cards. Call the cops. File an accident report.

"My poor car!" wails the woman. "It was my husband's car, and he loved it until the day he died! And now it's ruined!"

He takes a closer look at the woman, who has begun to sob. The tears seep down her cheeks from behind oversize mauve sunglasses that match the car's paint job. Her hands push through her thick, dark hair. She sags against the car's fender. "What'll I do? I've taken such good care of it since Vito died. And now look at it!"

Carl repeats to himself: Exchange driver's licenses. Produce insurance cards ....

"Look, lady, it'll be okay. I've got insurance. I'll make it right."

"Insurance?" she sobs. "But don't you see? This car is a 1989 model. They'll just total it. Oh, Vito, if only you were here. You always knew what exactly to do."

"The first thing we do is call the cops," Carl says. "We have to file an accident report. How do we find the cops in this burg?"

"You don't know anything, do you!" The Lincoln's driver stamps her foot. "Lousy snowbird! Y'all come down to Florida in packs and ruin it for us. Just look at what you've done. Aren't you ashamed?"

"Lady, it was an accident, that's all. I'm sorry."

"Well, tell your wife to get off her bottom and go into that Wal-Mart and look up the sheriff's number. Least she can do."

"I don't have a wife," says Carl.

"Then who's that blonde sitting on your front seat?"

"On the front seat?" Carl looks for himself. A crazed laugh builds in his throat. He can't quite stifle it. He giggles, then guffaws.

"What's so damn funny?" the woman demands.

Still chuckling, Carl walks over to Winnie's door and opens it. All ears and paws, Chester bounds out. The Town Car's driver stares, a sob choked off in midstream. Chester trots over to her, and she falls victim to his charm. She strokes his head. He lifts his chin, and she scratches him under his jaw.

Carl sees his chance. "All right," he says, "Chester can keep you company while I go find out how to reach the sheriff."

"No, wait," the woman says. She pulls off her sunglasses. For the first time, Carl gets a good look at her. He's already registered the thicket of curly brown hair, liberally streaked with gray. Though a trifle reddened by weeping, her brown eyes retain their luster. He disregards the crow's feet around them; after all, he's got them too. Her eyes look enormous in her small heart-shaped face. She's chewed most of her orange lipstick off her wide, full mouth. She's wearing pink slacks, a pink shirt and a pink sweater on a figure that's still buxom, if a bit settled.

"No wife?" she asks. "What's your name, bud?"

"Carl. Carl Swenson."

"Swede, eh? Don't you Scandahoovians like it better up where it's cold?"

"Dunno. Never been to Florida before."

"Oh. Well, it's a nice place. I've lived here all my life. Vito–my husband–came down from New Jersey. I was nineteen when we met. Handsome man he was, from a nice Italian family. He swept me off my feet. Good thing my mom and dad liked him too. Where are you from?"

At the side of the ring, Mother Nature snickers.

"Toledo," replies Carl. "My wife and I, well, we thought we'd stay there forever. But she died last year."

"I'm so sorry," she said, as though she meant it. "That's a shame."

Carl would not allow himself to be distracted. "Look here, these dents aren't so bad. A good body shop can pound them out, put on a little touch-up paint. Could have the car looking like new in no time. What's your name, by the way?"

"Rosemary Pascucci," she says, smiling a little. "My friends call me Rosie."

"Well, Mrs. Pascucci, do you know where we can find a decent body shop?"

"Nice body," she whispers, looking him over. "Oh, yeah, body shop, there's one in town."

Carl tries to ignore her scrutiny, but he can't help sucking in his gut and standing taller. "What town?"

"Bushnell, just up the road. Little place, good people. Not many snowbirds, 'cept in the RV parks."

Chester's forgetting his manners. He's rubbing up against her. Good idea, thinks Carl. "Bushnell. That where you live?"

"Nah, got a country place. Five acres. Out by the cattle ranches and the swamps. I just come to town for my groceries."

They're interrupted by a lanky kid sporting a Wal-Mart badge. Respectfully, he says to Mrs. Pascucci, "Ma'am, can you please move your car? It's blocking this lane and people need to use it to park."

"Oh, yes, move it." She flutters her hands helplessly, looking up at Carl. She's kind of short, he discovers. The top of her head barely reaches his shoulder.

"Mrs. Pascucci, I'll be happy to do it. What say we take it to that body shop of yours? I'll pay for the work." How much can it possibly cost, he thinks, out here in the middle of nowhere?

"I'd be pleased if you'd call me Rosie. Then you won't seem like such a stranger." She grabs the passenger door handle and then realizes the dented door won't open.

"Look, uh, Mrs., er, Rosie–you drive and I'll follow you in my toad–I mean my Focus. Suppose you go wait near the main road while I unhitch my car."

Rosie walks around her Lincoln and opens the door on the driver's side. Chester leaps into her car. Carl shakes his head and sets to work on the hitch. Soon he's following the mauve Town Car down the highway. Rosie leads him to a dirty little shop he wouldn't trust to fix a lawn mower. He asks the manager for an estimate. The manager hems and haws. Knowing a snowbird when he sees one, the manager names a figure that's way too high.

"Billy, you know I can't afford that kind of money," Rosie says, coming up next to Carl. She's fluttering her long mascara'd eyelashes at the manager. Helpless woman indeed, thinks Carl.

"Oh, so that's your car?" Billy asks.

"Ever since Vito died." She furrows her brow in a pitiful little frown.

Carl suspects Billy doesn't know Vito from a hole in the ground, but the manager caves in anyway. The price comes way down. Rosie eyes Carl.

"It's a deal," Carl agrees. "When can we–she–pick it up?"

"It's getting late, and I've got a couple of cars I gotta finish first. Tomorrow afternoon?"

Rosie hesitates. "I don't know how I'll get home."

"I'll be happy to drive you," Carl says. "C'mon, hop into my car. Chester!" The dog trots behind Rosie, tail wagging exuberantly.

"You're just so kind," says Rosie. "Let me at least buy you dinner at Red's Red Hot Barbecue.

Best ribs in town. Well, actually, the only ribs in town."

"I dunno. I've got to find a place for my Winnebago. Wal-Mart won't let RVs stay in their lots overnight anymore."

"I don't know if you noticed, but there's an RV park right next door to the Wal-Mart."

So there is. Carl takes a spot for a week. Who knows how long it will take to fix Rosie's car? Rosie stays with him through the negotiations with the park manager and looks on as he guides the Winnie into its assigned site.

Rosie seems in no hurry to go home. She watches, apparently rapt, as Carl hooks up the electricity, the water intake, the waste hoses and the cable TV. "I've never been inside one of these things," she says when he finishes. She climbs up the front steps with a switch of her hips.

Events are moving too fast for Carl. If he could, he'd just hitch up the toad, start Winnie's engine and retreat to Ohio, where ladies his age aren't inclined to get so familiar so fast. But he's already extended the Winnie's slideout, complete with its comfortable sofa, and there's Rosie, already enthroned upon the cushions.

Carl gives up. Smiling tentatively, he offers, "I've got a steak in the fridge and a bottle of nice wine. Why don't I make us some dinner?"

While Carl chops onions and mushrooms to go with the steak, Rosie explores the Winnie. "What a cute little stove," she exclaims over the three-burner propane range. "A real refrigerator! And a CD player! Got any good music?"

"In the cabinet over there." He points. She opens a closet instead. A stray wool sweater falls out.

"You sure won't need this in Florida," she says, holding the sweater at arm's length. "Least not 'til January. It can get cold down here, though. One year it even snowed. Course it melted right away."

Finally she finds the packet of CDs and slides one into the player. It's an old Neil Diamond recording. Carl thought he'd given it away. He never liked Neal Diamond, but he remembers that this record used to put Janice into a loving mood. Now it reminds him of the good times.

While the steak sizzles, Carl nukes a couple of potatoes and a bowlful of green peas. The wine's a pleasant red, nothing fancy. He uncorks it and fills two plastic cups. Handing Rosie her cup, he raises the other. "Cheers," he says.

"Cheers to you too," she smiles. "To a really nice snowbird."

The meal over, Rosie feeds Chester the scraps. Carl puts the dishes in the sink. He washes, she dries.

"It's dark out," Carl says. "I should be taking you home." He digs in his pocket for the toad's keys.

Rosie grabs him in a surprise hug. "You've been so good to me!" The hug is close and warm. She's soft, the way he likes his women. He tries a kiss. She doesn't resist. It's a long kiss, and tongues become involved. Then she breaks away, giggling, and flops down on the big bed.

"My, this is comfortable. I never thought one of these trailers–

"RV," Carl corrects her.

"Yeah. One of these RVs. I never thought they'd be so nice. Or maybe it's the company."

Inside Carl a big hard lump of northern ice begins to thaw. "Rosie, you're a sweet woman. I like you." He stretches out on the bedspread beside her. Chester curls up at the foot of the bed.

During the night, a pounding rain awakens Carl. He hears water dripping on the carpet beside the bed–his side. He remembers the caulk he didn't buy. Now's not the time to worry about it, though. He scoots over, snuggles up against Rosie's back. She murmurs contentedly.

Winter has come to Florida, has seen, has been conquered. The orange groves are safe. The magnetic Scotties, against all odds, cuddle close. The Montagues and Capulets set their seal on a love match.

Under the covers, Carl begins contemplating a Florida future.

Mother Nature winks at the audience. Then she steps out of the ring and vanishes into the warm, rainy night.

Potter's Field

Dalia Lindstrom scanned the crowded student cafeteria in the Toledo Museum of Art's School of Art and Design, looking for Charley Robideau. Robideau, a renowned ceramic artist, had taught at the museum school for years, while Dalia had just begun teaching. She had been pleased and flattered when he invited her to lunch. At 35, she had achieved considerable recognition for her mosaics, but she was hardly in the same league as Robideau.

Robideau's gruff voice carried over the noise of the crowd. "Hey, Dalia," she heard him call, "grab a couple of sandwiches for us–I'll take ham and turkey and a black coffee–and come join me." Dalia saw him settled at a table near the back wall, a small man with dark eyes and silver-streaked black hair. "I'd get the food myself, but somebody has to hold this table for us," he said.

Dalia sniffed. A gentleman would have let her sit down and gone for the food himself. She considered telling Robideau so and then decided against it. He looked rather thin and frail. Perhaps he was ailing. Besides, his was the superior talent and the superior reputation, so he had a right to his quirks. She picked up the sandwich for him and a salad for herself.

Through a half-chewed mouthful of ham and turkey, Robideau mumbled, "Now, my dear, tell me about your mosaics. I find your images of griffins and sphinxes and pagan gods to be most compelling. They're fascinating folkloric motifs."

Dalia warmed to the man. "It started when I was in art school," she explained. "I signed up for a folklore course. The old myths and religions seized my imagination and demanded expression. I was painting in oils then, but my style was too realistic to convey the essence of the supernatural beings I envisioned. That's when I switched to mosaics. Mosaics require that the artist subtract detail, which encourages abstraction. That abstraction forces viewers to use their imaginations and bring forth their own ideas of the divine."

"And you use bits of glass for your tiles?" Robideau inquired.

Dalia nodded. "Yes, glass and earthenware and china. On recycling days I go prowling for materials in curbside bins of discarded bottles. And I haunt thrift shops and yard sales, anywhere I might find unusual colors and designs in glass and ceramic."

"I'd like to talk more about it," said Robideau thoughtfully. "Would you consider visiting me at my studio?"

Dalia blinked. "Well, of course I'd love to," she said. "Your ceramics are some of the most beautiful objects I've ever seen. I'd like to see how you work– but your preference for solitude is legendary. Why are you offering me an invitation?" Dalia was fairly sure Robideau wasn't making a pass at her. She wasn't the kind of woman who attracted men, not pretty and soft. Instead, she was tall and big-boned, with a broad Nordic face and eyes set too close together. And Robideau was at least twenty years older than she. So what did he want?

"I might have an ulterior motive or two, but nothing you can't handle," Robideau told her. "Would you like to come Saturday? My place is way out south along the Maumee River, but it's a lovely drive most days, even now when there's snow on the ground."

"Saturday? Yes, I could do that," Dalia ventured.

"Come for brunch, then. I'll even cook–scrambled eggs, bacon, cinnamon rolls, all that grand food the experts say isn't good for us. But maybe you could bring the cinnamon rolls–unless you don't mind the refrigerated kind that come in a can."

Dalia smiled. "I know a very nice bakery in Grand Rapids, where I live." She rose from the table. "I need to get ready for my class now. I'll see you Saturday morning."

On Saturday, as she'd promised, Dalia bought a dozen cinnamon rolls and then steered her van south along the river road. Some twenty miles beyond Grand Rapids, she found Robideau's place, a large old farmhouse perched on a bluff overlooking the broad river. As she parked and turned off her engine, she spotted Robideau on the front porch, waving her in.

He accepted the box of cinnamon rolls from her. "Still warm, are they? Perfect! Brunch will be ready in a jiffy."

Robideau might not have been much of a baker, but his scrambled eggs with mushrooms were superb, and the bacon was expertly crisped. The coffee was strong and black, just the way Dalia liked it. Then Robideau opened a bottle of champagne–with artistic finesse, Dalia noted, easing the cork out rather than letting it pop.

"To a fine young artist with a stellar future ahead." Robideau raised his glass to her.

"Thank you," she replied, looking down and sipping from her glass to hide her discomfiture. She was a competent artist, she knew, but not a great one.

When they'd finished their champagne, they headed for Robideau's studio. Dalia had seen enough of Robideau's pieces to know that whatever he was working on would be exceptional. He could throw perfectly symmetrical bowls, vases and urns, which he reshaped when they came off the wheel, creating unexpected forms that took viewers by surprise. He was known for the color, depth and sheen of his glazes. He formulated them himself, and they were his particular pride.

Inside the studio, row upon row of shelves contained finished work; many more held pieces awaiting their turn in the kiln. The more Dalia saw of Robideau's work, the more inadequate she felt. She told him so.

"I'm far from perfect, my dear," Robideau replied. "I've made more artistic blunders in my lifetime than you'll ever commit. Here, come see."

She followed him out the door. He pointed to a pasture near the studio. It was full of overgrown hillocks that sparkled in the sunlight. "Dalia, do you know what a potter's field is?"

"No," Dalia shook her head.

Robideau explained, "The gospel of Matthew tells us that Judas repented his betrayal of Jesus and tried to return the thirty pieces of silver to the chief priests and elders. When they refused the money, Judas threw it down and went away to hang himself. The priests bought the potter's field with the silver and used it as a place to bury foreigners.

"Since then, burial grounds for strangers and the indigent–society's failures–are often called potters' fields," Robideau continued. "I'm a potter who makes a lot of unsuccessful pots. I take them into that pasture and smash them on top of my other failures, where they remind me that I'm fallible. And that's my potter's field."

The glowing colors and lusters of the broken pots drew Dalia to look more closely. Picking up a handful of shards, she asked Robideau, "Would you mind if I were to use some of these broken pieces in my mosaics?"

"They're no use to me," Robideau said. "You can have whatever you like, but in return you must promise to visit me often. I like you, and I have so little company these days."

Why not? Dalia thought. I might learn a lot from this man.

"I could come on Saturdays, like today," she said. She kept her word, sharing weekend meals with Robideau, whom she learned to call Charley as they spent hours talking about art and life. Under Charley's influence, her art developed greater forcefulness and power. He helped her gain entree into new galleries, and her mosaics were selling well.

As spring eased into summer and summer into fall, Charley grew thinner and more frail. He made fewer pieces, and although he still prepared meals for her visits, he ate less and less. Dalia was worried, but she was too polite to probe into his health. She felt it was none of her business.

On a warm Saturday in early October, Dalia entered Charley's house to find that the artist had built a fire in the fieldstone fireplace and was huddled in his armchair in front of it. Dalia squatted in front of him and took his hands. They were icy. She said, "Come on, Charley, you've always had enough energy for two. What's wrong?"

Charley grimaced. "I haven't wanted to tell you this, but now I have no choice. I have a cancer that is destroying my blood and bones. I don't have much longer to live."

"You can't die," Dalia protested. "The art world needs you. You're one of a kind, and no other ceramic artist even comes close to you. Besides, you're my mentor, my cheering section and my best friend. You have to keep on living."

"No, my dear, it just can't be," Charley said wearily. "I've achieved almost everything I wanted, skill and fame and wealth. There is just one thing more that's kept me going, only one goal that's eluded me, but I understand now that I won't achieve it before I die."

"What could that possibly be?" Dalia felt compelled to ask.

"I long to create the absolutely perfect pot," Charley said, "a piece fit for the gods you depict so well in your mosaics. I believe I've come close, now and again. But I should have known that the gods never allow true perfection in mortals."

"You still have time." Dahlia tried to comfort him. "I'll move in with you, take care of your house and make dinners for you, and then you'll have strength enough to continue working."

"I never thought I'd have to ask you for help, Dalia," Charley replied. "But I'd be grateful if you stayed with me for awhile. You have become the love of my life."

Following that conversation, Dalia moved in with Charley and worked on her pieces in Charley's studio while he watched her from his wheelchair. Then one November day, Dalia realized that Charley's life could be measured in mere hours. She stepped outside, her throat swollen with grief, and wandered over to Charley's field of failed pots.

As she walked, Dalia discovered an overgrown heap she had never noticed before. She pulled away the weeds that covered it. Under the withered foliage she discovered a pot half-buried in the black loam. With her bare hands, she scraped the dirt away from it, unearthing an intact piece in the shape of a ginger jar. Her fingers glided easily over its surface. Its swelling curves perfectly communicated the shaping hand of its maker. Digging deeper into the hole where the jar had rested, Dalia found the lid. Both pieces were glazed with something that felt as smooth as spider silk. Charley had finished the piece in shades of teal, ranging from a dark hue on the neck of the vessel, a bright pale tone on the belly of the jar and the darkest hue on the footed base.

Dalia held the jar up into the sunlight, revealing silver motes flashing brilliantly within the depths of the glaze, and she knew that this was the perfect piece Charley had spent his life trying to create.

She took the jar into the house and placed it on the table beside Charley's bed.

"Where did you find this?" Charley whispered.

"In your potter's field," Dalia told him.

"Let me see it," Charley said. Dalia placed the jar into his outstretched hands. He stroked its rounded surfaces, studying its shape and its colors. "Five years ago I made this. I couldn't bear to destroy it. But I had to get it out of my sight. If I'd kept it in the light of day, I would never have made another piece."

"But you said you were still striving for the perfect pot," protested Dalia.

"Maybe I meant–I meant striving for the sake of this perfect pot." Charley's eyes closed.

"Dalia, please bury my ashes in this jar," he murmured. "Bury them at the edge of my field. You know the spot."

Dalia nodded. "I will," she promised. But seeds of betrayal, little leaden flecks, had sprouted in her soul. It galled her to think that this beautiful jar would soon be interred with its creator and never seen again.

At Charley's funeral mass, fellow artists, students past and present, and friends from the art world overflowed the pews and spilled into the aisles. But the potter had no family to claim his ashes. Dalia had them sealed into an urn provided by the funeral home. She took the urn back to Charley's house and placed it on a table next to the silver-flecked teal jar. Looking at the urn and the pot side by side, she convinced herself that she was doing the right thing: Charley's perfect creation could not be allowed to vanish from the sight of the living.

Rising the next morning in a cloudy dawn, Dalia took a spade from Charley's garden shed and began digging at the spot Charley had chosen for his grave. It didn't take long to excavate a pit deep enough for the funerary urn–she was strong, and the black Ohio dirt was soft.

When the grave was ready, Dalia placed the urn in it. Carefully she shoveled the dirt back into the grave until a low mound of soft earth rose above it. Come spring, tender young grass would clothe Charley Robideau's resting place. He had sought no greater memorial. Knowing that, Dalia knelt beside the freshly turned earth and prayed to all the gods she knew that they would honor his soul.

Inside Charley's house, the teal jar waited. Dalia packed it up along with her tools, her boxes of potsherds and mosaics she had not yet finished. She loaded everything into her van and headed for home.

Back in her own studio, Dalia positioned Charley's teal jar on a stand in the very center of her work space. She opened the curtains to let the sunlight awaken the depths of its glaze. Its silvered motes sparkled.

Then she looked around the room, where she displayed many of her mosaics. She was horrified. They were dull, plain and uninspired, all of them, as her life would be now that Charley was dead.

Struck by an insight, Dalia paused in her evaluation. Yes, her works seemed plain, but only by comparison to the glorious perfection of Charley's jar. If she looked at each of her pieces singly, comparing them only to her private vision, they were wondrous indeed. Why had she never realized this?

Dalia reached a decision. She packed up Charley's perfect work and drove back to his place. On the road, she noticed for the first time in months how the sunlight danced on the Maumee's rapids. It reminded her of the shimmering motes in the teal jar's glaze, yet far surpassed their earthbound beauty. The blue-green of the sky along the horizon recalled Charley's lustered teal, but the depth of the color far exceeded that of the jar's glossy surface.

The gods have little patience with mortal pretensions to perfection.

Back at Charley's place, Dalia carried the jar to the fresh grave. "Take back the perfect beauty that's yours, Charley Robideau," she said. "I'll be embarking on my own quest for perfection, in memory of you, beloved."

And she drove the blade of the shovel once more into the raw earth.

The Water Horse

Ellie MacRae followed the deer trail that climbed the ridge alongside Hellfire Creek, the fast-rushing stream that spilled out from Devil's Pond. The country people insisted that the pond was bottomless, its waters welling up from hell itself.

Anyone who had grown up in the Tennessee mountains, as Ellie had, understood that the world contained beings and forces that no scientist could account for. She did not find it odd that she heard voices in the night wind. Once, when she was quite young, Ellie had witnessed a naked man crowned with antlers striding among the trees. Many years later she learned that the ancient Celts had revered an antlered manlike creature as a god. The revelation didn't surprise her.

But the tales about Hellfire Creek and Devil's Pond were too far-fetched even for Ellie's quirky mind. Suppose she granted the possibility that the water might flow from Old Scratch's realm. Then where was the heat? Surely water from hell would boil, like the hot springs in Yellowstone. The stench of brimstone? The water from many a local well exuded the sulfurous odor of rotten eggs, but the mountain pool was cold and clear in all seasons, and the water tasted sweet and pure.

So the tales could not be true. Nor the other stories either, of unearthly music that a late-night wanderer who ventured too close to the pool might hear. So the superstitious local people avoided the creek and the pond, allowing Ellie the solitude she cherished. Before she went away to college, she often came to this place, her banjo slung across her back. A large boulder emerged from the earth beside the pool, and she sat on it for hours, playing the old mountain tunes her grandfather had taught her.

This day, the final day of October, the morning had dawned unusually warm. Soon the winter cold would descend and strip from the trees those golden leaves that blanketed the slopes with their ephemeral glory. As she pulled on a pair of faded blue jeans and a well-worn blue shirt, Ellie had eyed the stack of math tests awaiting correction. Today was Saturday, and surely duty could wait. She would allow herself time to take in all that beauty.

Ellie made herself a cup of coffee and went out to the porch of her little cabin, where she sat down

in a chair that her great-grandfather had built for Ellie's mother. Her mother had passed the chair down
to her, along with a scrap of worn quilt to cushion it.

Thinking of her mother still brought tears. Less
than two months ago, her mother had died. Ellie had
expected it, but that didn't make the death any eas-
ier. During the days, she could manage. In September, she had started her teaching job, her first post
since she had finished her degree. She'd been hired
at the new school in Clinton, thirty minutes' drive
from her isolated valley. She'd been nearly overwhelmed by the rambunctious fourth-graders and
the busywork that went with her teaching job, but
the work kept her mind off her grief.

Ellie let her gaze wander the familiar slopes. If
she looked carefully through the screening trees, she
could make out a gleam of sunlight reflected on the
surface of Devil's Pond. A breeze gusted, bringing
down a shower of leaves. She inhaled their hot, dry
aroma, the scent bearing the conviction of autumn.

Ellie finished her coffee, reminding herself that
the children's math tests awaited. Then she
shrugged. The day held too much beauty to spend
with her eyes focused on the wavering, hesitant
numbers the children had scrawled.

Reentering her cabin, she piled ham, cheese and
lettuce onto a slice of bread. Coating a second slice
with a film of mustard, she completed the sandwich
and wrapped it in wax paper like her Ma used to do.
Tucking it into her shirt pocket, she picked up her
banjo and slung its strap over her shoulder. Stepping out onto the porch once more, she firmly
latched the cabin door behind her.

Ellie arrived at Devil's Pond near noon. She slipped out from under her banjo strap and leaned the instrument against a tree stump, admiring it for a moment. She'd been almost twelve when she got it. By that age, she was playing reels and hornpipes on her grandfather's old Sears Roebuck banjo, backing up her father's intricate fiddling.

Her mother had scolded her when Ellie slipped away to the barn, banjo in hand, with the dishes only half-dried. "Ellen Rachel MacRae, a girl who plays the banjo is likely to come to a bad end. Everybody knows it's the devil's own instrument." But Ma smiled when she said it. She liked the music as well as anyone.

One day Ellie's father and her grandfather had taken her to a music store in Knoxville. She saw the banjo she wanted right away. With mother of pearl designs inset into its peg head and its ebony fingerboard, it was a pretty thing. It had been more costly than her family had counted on, but when her grandfather heard her play "Over the Waterfall" on it there in the store, he smiled and reached deeper into his pockets. She'd played that banjo ever since.

Sitting down on the poolside rock, Ellie unwrapped her sandwich and bit into it, savoring the smoky flavor of country ham and the prickly bite of the mustard. When she finished the sandwich, Ellie filled an empty plastic bottle with water from the pool and drank. The water tasted even better than she'd remembered it, reminding her of clover honey and mint.

Ellie set the bottle down on the moss beside her rock and picked up the banjo. With the twist of a couple of pegs, she had it tuned and ready. She started off simply with "Old Joe Clark" and "Sally Ann," songs that must have traveled across the Atlantic with the Scots-Irish who had settled these hills so long ago. Gradually she worked her way up to the complex figures of "The Falls of Richmond," hearing in her mind her father's fiddling as she played. Both Dad and Granddad were gone now, at rest in the little Baptist cemetery in the valley below. A few weeks ago, almost two years to the day after Dad's death, Ellie had watched the gravediggers lay Ma down to rest beside Dad. Her older brother and sister had moved north, to Chicago. That's where the good jobs were, they said. She seldom heard from them. Ellie was the only one of the family content to live in the hills.

Ellie had just started into the second part of "West Fork Girls" when a vigorous splashing from the pool broke the music's spell. She looked out over the pond, where ripples were still spreading. In the very center, a head broke water, followed by bare brown shoulders. The rivulets that spilled from tangles of dark hair and streamed down a bronzed face did nothing to conceal the fact that the head's owner was masculine. Ellie stared, appalled that this person — this man — had profaned her sacred space.

"Hey, lady," he called out. "I left my clothes behind the rock you're sittin' on. How'm I supposed to get out and dry off with you starin' at me?"

"What are you doing here?" Ellie demanded to know. "This is my spot."

"Do you own this land?"

"Of course not. It's a state forest," she replied through compressed lips.

"Yeah, well, then, it's as much my spot as it is yours, ain't it?" The man spoke with the soft slurred drawl of the hill folk. "I'm gettin' cold here in the water. Mind lookin' the other way while I get out? You can keep playin' that thing. Just look away for a minute, okay?"

"Okay," Ellie agreed. She didn't have much choice. He'd probably come out whether she looked or not. So she shifted her seat until her back was turned and waited.

Ellie wouldn't have been normal if she hadn't stolen a sideways look. She glimpsed a sturdy, well-muscled body, on the tall side, she thought.

"You promised not to look," he complained, and she hastily bent to her banjo, playing a very loud, very percussive rendition of "Red Haired Boy," over and over until the stranger approached, pushing shaggy black hair away from his forehead. He had donned a black shirt, tight black trousers and tall black boots. He held a black cowboy hat in his hand, waving it in the air as he bowed to her in mock politeness.

"Who do you think you are, some kind of two-bit Johnny Cash?" she asked sourly.

He laughed. He had black eyes that sparkled. "I don't know no Johnny Cash. My name's Rob. But you just might be surprised at who I am. Did anybody ever tell you you're a pretty thing? Or you would be if you'd only smile."

"That's about the most feeble pickup line I've ever heard." Ellie shook her head and bent over her banjo again. She started in on a drop-thumb riff, but her concentration was shot. "I've seen plenty of guys

who are better looking than you are, and one of them
wants to marry me."

Now why had she felt compelled to say that? It
was true, at least the part about better-looking guys.
This man, who appeared to be just a little older than
she, was rather coarse-featured, with a long nose
and a wide mouth set in a squared-off face. Rough
trade, her Ma would have said. But he had nice eyes.
As for the man who wanted to marry her, he was
assuredly better looking than this one. He was also
a prig. Still, Ellie had been thinking lately that he
might do. She wasn't getting any younger.

"Play for me awhile, will ya?" The stranger's
voice held a pleading note. "I love music, and it's
been a coon's age since I heard a good banjo. Used
to be a lot of 'em around here, but all them old folk
that used to play are gone now."

Ellie sighed. She'd wanted this day to herself.
But she could never disappoint an eager audience,
so she started playing again. Just a few phrases into
the tune, she heard the first sharp bow strokes of a
fiddle taking the lead part. She looked up. Her new
acquaintance held the instrument against his shoulder in the old style, sawing at the strings and tapping his foot. Together, they played the old songs as
well as she and her dad had ever done. Before she
knew it, the sun dropped below the mountaintops,
and mist began rising up out of the valley.

"I've got to go home now," Ellie announced.

"Do you?" The man who called himself Rob laid
his fiddle on the rock and took her banjo from her.
"I thought maybe—well, you looked lonely. So'm I.
Stay awhile yet?"

Ellie moved closer to him, not knowing why. He reached out with one hand, gently untangling a few windblown strands of her chestnut hair. She edged into his kiss. He tasted like water from the pool, like clover honey and mint.

"Ah, but no, a fine gal like you, you're not for the likes of me." Rob drew away.

Ellie felt unaccountably disappointed.

"Get on my back, and I'll take you away from here," Ellie heard Rob say, and she didn't think for a minute he meant to escort her home. Where the man had been stood a tall black horse. She saw all too clearly that he was a stallion.

Right then Ellie knew her Ma had been right about girls who played banjos coming to a bad end. The dark animal who confronted her was a kelpie, a shape-shifting demon that lurked in rivers and lakes — and ponds. If she got on his back, he would gallop away with her and never stop running until she died. And then he would eat her. This was the tale as the old folk related it. Indeed, her grandfather had told her that a friend of his youth, brash Jake Gillespie, had been seen mounting such a horse, and no one ever saw him again. A line from an old song echoed in her mind: "If you go, you can't come back."

"Sling your banjo over your shoulder and climb on," a voice that seemed to come from the horse insisted. It was Rob's voice, though it had lost its good ol' boy drawl. "King Finnvara — he who rules the fairy court — has heard of your music, and he would welcome your presence in his hall. For in this land, our people are few, and short of musicians. You'd grace our court in fine style."

Ellie tried to stay rational. She heard herself say, "But the school. My pupils. I can't just leave them. Oh, dear God, I don't believe I'm talking to a horse."

The dark equine shape faded into the shadows, revealing the man again. "If you truly wish to stay, I won't force you to come. But why say no before you have met the king? You will have until dawn to make up your mind."

The words rang in Ellie's head: *If you go, you can't come back.* Yet, in the afterglow of the sunset, she nodded.

Rob knelt before her. "Place your hands on my shoulders," he said, and then Ellie found herself atop the water horse's back. She wrapped both arms around his neck and held on as he leaped into a gallop. They flew through the high meadows and dodged the forest trees until the moon rose high and full. At last they emerged into a moonlit glade encircled by ancient thick-boled trees. The horse slowed and then stopped, bowing down so that Ellie might slip off his back. In the next moment, the horse vanished and Rob the man, wearing a black tunic belted over black leggings, stood beside her once more. His shaggy hair fell down over his brow. His fiddle rested on his left shoulder, and his right hand held the bow at the ready.

"Let's play our music again, together," Rob said, and Ellie took her banjo from her back and tuned it.

Ellie started playing slowly, intending to pick a simple old tune. Instead, something new emerged from her fingers, music she had no recollection of ever hearing before. Rob joined in, the sweet notes of the fiddle soaring over the steady beat of her banjo.

At the perimeter of Ellie's vision shadows emerged from the trees into the flower-dappled glade. Moving with the rhythm, the amorphous shapes gradually solidified, taking on the semblance of humans, but taller, brighter, more graceful. Both male and female, they wore garments as airy and colorful as the petaled meadow. The scents of sandalwood, jasmine, and neroli, dizzying in their fragrance, rose from the grass under their feet.

Ellie felt clumsy and plain in her shirt and jeans. Who was she to perform in the presence of such otherworldly creatures? Her hands threatened to tremble, disastrous for a musician. But her water horse smiled at her and picked up the music's pace. She followed him with unexpected ease. The dancers whirled and spun in time to the music's insistent pulse.

Ellie and the kelpie played until the sky paled in the false dawn. Then one of the beautiful men approached her. He wore a silken jacket and hose as silvery as the moon overhead. A diadem sparkling with gems crowned his pale gilt hair, and she knew he must be the fairies' king. Rob set aside his fiddle and offered to take her banjo from her, but she clung to it as though it were her last link to the world she knew. Rob took a step back.

"Ellen Rachel MacRae, I am called Finnvara, and it is I who have sent for you," said the silvered king, bowing his glittering head to her. "We of Faerie thank you for your music this night."

"But—but—there can't be fairies in Tennessee," Ellie objected. "If there ever were any in the world, they must have been left behind across the ocean. No one has ever seen a fairy in America."

"Have they not? Perhaps they mistook us for ghosts or spirits. But here you are among us. Can you not see what we are?" Indeed Finnvara was too solid to be a ghost, too beautiful to be human. So, in truth, were the others, all except for Rob, the kelpie who had carried her here. In Rob she sensed a spirit and a warmth that the ethereal dancers lacked. His looks had improved when he entered his own world, but they were still rough. He was also a horse. Of sorts.

"Yes, I see," Ellie answered. "I think I do. But you're like something out of a Walt Disney movie."

"I don't know what a Walt Disney movie is," said the silvery man, eyes as gray and clear as the dawning sky focused upon her own ordinary blue ones.

"No, I suppose you don't. You don't live in the same world as I do, do you?"

"I don't," said the beautiful king of Faerie. "My world lies next to yours. But tonight is one of the few nights of the year that our worlds touch. I can enter yours, and you can come to mine. Will you stay and play your music for us until time ends? In my world you will never know pain, nor the sorrow that is the lot of your kind. You may wed one of us, one who would be handsome and kind beyond all your dreams."

As he spoke, seven tall men, almost as handsome and regal as Finnvara himself, ranged themselves in a row facing Ellie. "Look upon your suitors," the king commanded. "Which of these would you choose?"

Ellie's mouth fell open. Of course she was tempted. But what if it was all a lie? What if indeed Devil's Pond sprang straight from hell and she had just played her music for the fallen angels?

The kelpie-man nudged her. "You can go home again. It's not yet too late."

"Robin!" barked the king. His face changed to something harder, something dangerous. "I warned you, she is not for you. You are only a messenger, a lowly kelpie. She is destined for the high court of Faerie. Already you have interfered too much. I could have you flayed. Obey me, or you will nevermore walk the worlds as either horse or man."

"So your true name is Robin," said Ellie, facing the kelpie. "Now that I know it, do I hold your fate in my hands? Or does this cruel being who calls himself a king?"

"You do, my sweet musician." The rough-looking water horse glared at his king. "You hold the power of choice. You can do as Finnvara says and choose for yourself any one of these glorious men of Faerie. I'll go back to my mountain pool and pine for your music. Or you can return home, but you'll never come back to my dwelling. You'll remember all this only as a mildly pleasant dream. But I'll not forget you, Ellie, not for all time."

"Ellen, you must decide before the sun rises," said the stern king of the fairies. "If you leave us, you will never return. If you are still here when the dawn light appears, you must stay with us forever."

Ellie loved her familiar life–or did she? Did she truly want to teach ungrateful children lessons they didn't want to learn and listen to their even more

ungrateful parents complain when their little dar-
lings didn't get top marks? Should she marry not for
love but for practicality? Did she want a short and
prosaic life and then submit herself to the grave?

But what awaited her in this strange new
world? The devil's own offspring? Fairies with
beautiful faces and hearts hard and black as Cumberland coal? Would she be damned to an eternity
in which to regret her choice?

"Look at me," said Rob. "I'm no handsome
prince, and no kiss will transform me into one. I'm
just a kelpie, immortal, but still one of the lesser creatures in Faerie. But I ask you to look at me anyway."

Ellie did, stared into black eyes merry and deep
by turns.

"Now listen." Rob raised his fiddle to his shoulder and began to play songs she had never heard before, songs of unspeakable beauty, full of strength
and love. She lifted her banjo. "No," he said. "Just
listen. I am playing for you and only you, you who
came to my pool for so many years and played for
me, even though you did not know I was there. Listen."

And listen she did, transported, until the rays of
the sun topped the mountains and her fate was
sealed.

In the glow of that otherworldly morning,
Robin laid his fiddle down and waited. Ellie looked
around at the unearthly glory of the men of Faerie,
and she chose. She reached a hand out to her kelpie,
and he took it. "Not just a kelpie," she whispered.
"My Robin."

An excited murmur arose from the fairy gathering when she spoke the kelpie's true name.

Ellie turned to face Finnvara. "You may not harm my Robin," she said defiantly. "I have claimed him. He is yours no more."

The silver king threw back his glorious head and laughed, a miraculous sound like the chiming of harp strings. "Mortal, you have fairly won your faerie prince. Your love for Robin compels me to forgive his transgression. Let all here witness that Ellen Rachel MacRae and Robin, our kelpie, are now wed. They will play their music for us forever. Let us drink to the magic of their love."

Clear crystalline goblets appeared, brimful of a rosy liquid. Robin took one from Finnvara's hands and offered it to Ellie. She sipped carefully, tasting clover honey and mint and something more, the intoxicating flavor of a new life. Then she gave the goblet to the kelpie, and he drank in his turn, his dark eyes looking over the rim into hers.

The sun rose higher, and the fairies glided into invisibility among the trees. All but Robin. "I know a bank where the wild thyme blows," he said. "We shall make our marriage bed among oxlips and violets, among sweet musk-roses and eglantine."

"You've stolen that from William Shakespeare," said Ellie.

"No, Shakespeare stole it from us." The kelpie-man took on the semblance of the black horse and knelt beside Ellie. Banjo in hand, she mounted. He sprang into a gallop, abandoning the enchanted glade for the wild mountainsides of Faerie.

Ellie understood at last that the old tales were right. Her Robin, her water horse, her kelpie, would carry her away, and she would never be seen in Tennessee again. The reassuring words of another old

ballad came to her: "I know where I'm going, and I know who's going with me. I know who I love..."
    She hoped she did.

The Wedding at Tommy Knocker's
Cavern Tavern

"Hey!" Ragna burst into Tommy's Knocker's Cavern Tavern, her bulk threatening to fracture the stalactite pillars framing the bar's entrance. Two bedraggled goblins, less than half her six-foot stature, trailed behind her. "Look what I brought you, Tommy — a pair of lovers fresh from the tunnels under Chicago, looking to get married among their own kind."

Ragna was Tommy's barmaid, had been for more than a century as humans reckoned time. She was a troll, widowed since her husband, Sven, out hunting one night, had been caught in a thunder-storm. The dark clouds deceived him into thinking he had enough time left before dawn to return to the caves under the western Wisconsin hills. He was almost home when the clouds parted and a sunbeam turned him to stone. Sven's granite form stood eternally on guard outside the tavern's entrance to the outside world. Every summer evening, Ragna gathered bouquets of flowers to place in his outstretched, pleading hands, and in winter she gave him nosegays of icicles.

Tommy gave the bedraggled pair of goblins a sidelong glance. "Where'd you get them?"

"Found 'em out in the cornfield. They 'as lookin' for us. This here's Ripshin."

The male goblin, a right handsome sort as goblins go, touched the brim of his ragged cap respectfully. "Beggin' your pardon, Mr. Knocker. We wouldna troubled you, but tis raining out."

"And t'other be Raphine." For a goblin, Raphine was downright pretty, with a triangular face and black hair that looked to be long, though it was all tangled and dripping wet.

"What's a tavern for, if not to be a home away from home?" Ragna slipped behind the bar and filled two steins from the tap. "You two be just in time for some Huber bock. You can only get Hubie bock in the spring, ya know — that be when the brewmasters drain the vats. The best stuff be down there in the bottom. Them Huber people been in these hills long enough to know they'd best give Tommy the best bock first. If they don't, Tommy and his knockers will turn it sour."

"Whoa." Ripshin took a sip from his stein. "I thought knockers was supposed to be in the mines — you know, to warn miners if there's a cave-in a-coming."

At the far end of the bar, at the end of a line of trolls and gnomes, a pair of kobold buddies huddled over brimming steins of Leinenkugel — Tunx and Scrag. Like the knockers, kobolds were mine sprites. The knockers had followed their Cornish humans across the ocean to Wisconsin's lead mines; the kobolds had accompanied their German miners.

Tunx looked up. He was red-eyed by nature, the more so since he'd been imbibing pint after pint of Leinie. "Ain't so many mines as there used to be. Not so bad. Gives us more time to drink." He caught sight of Raphine. "By Odin and his eight-legged steed, I ain't seen nuthin' so pretty since I left the Black Forest. Hey, beautiful lady —" He leered in her direction.

Ragna turned a broad scowl on him. "She be engaged, you ugly fool, to this fine goblin gentleman. She's not for the likes of a scraggly tunnel rat like you."

"Don't talk to me about ugly, you troll." Tunx thrust his stein at her. "Give the lady a pint from me, and don't forget Scrag here He be needin' a refill too." He plunked a tiny garnet on the bar in payment as Scrag smiled gratefully. "And keep the change."

At the other end of the bar, Ripshin bristled and rolled up his sleeves. "I didn't come here to have my gal insulted by a clod like you."

"Now, now." Tommy spoke soothingly. "No quarrels here, understand? This be Tommy

Knocker's Cavern Tavern, where mountain folk gather to greet and mate. You two fine goblins have matin' in mind, right? What be stoppin' you?"

Ripshin downed his Hubie bock in one long draw and placed a big amethyst on the bar. "Tale-tellin' be thirsty work. I'll have a refill—and this'll pay for Raphine's next glass too. She don't accept drinks from strangers."

"Won't be strangers long. You'll see." Tunx glared sullenly from his end of the bar.

Ripshin accepted another foaming stein from Tommy. "See, there be this goblin marriage custom. We prize emeralds above all other gems. Emeralds make for lasting love. So for me to wed me darlin' properly, I must give her an emerald. A big one. Now there be emeralds in Chicago—stores full of emeralds and other gems. But not a single one fine enough for a goblin bride. I searched the rocks two hundred feet below the buildings and even under Lake Michigan, but it be all limestone, and you don't never find emeralds in limestone."

"It be mostly limestone here too." Tommy slapped the polished bar. "This be flowstone, you see, and the bar stools be calcite stalagmites, and the lovely wall behind the bar be a row of stalactites."

"Indeed the wall looks like organ pipes. Lovely sight." Ripshin sighed. "I tunneled into a church by accident oncet. That be how I know. By the way, I must congratulate you on the fine pictures you've got on that wall."

"Can't have mirrors, you know. You goblins be handsome enough, but most of my patrons be cave cretins. They see themselves in a mirror, and, well, they get downright frightened. So I persuaded some

Winnebago Indians from the reservation above ground to paint pictures of us on the walls — prettied up, of course. We sprinkled cave dust in their eyes when they finished so they couldn't find their way back, but I paid 'em handsomely with gold nuggets."

"Not much gold in Wisconsin, so I hear tell." Ripshin smiled. "But word among the Chicago fairies is that there be a dragon in these hills — with a hoard that has lots of big emeralds. Probably gold too, eh?"

At the end of the bar, Tunx waved frantically at Tommy, placing a finger across his lips for silence. Ripshin saw and nodded. "So it be true."

Ragna patted Tommy's shoulder affectionately. "It be true, all right. But Groseclose don't take kindly to strangers tryin' to steal his treasure. He be a real firebreather, that one. We bake our Cornish pasties in a rock oven heated by the dragon fire, and we're almost a mile away from Groseclose's den." She opened a wooden door in the wall of the tavern. A cloud of steam spilled out. She retrieved two plump pasties from the cavity and put them on a plate, setting it down in front of the goblin couple. "Dragon fire's worth more than dragon treasure, if you ask me. Just taste how well old Groseclose baked these succulent pasties. Pretty stones be all right, but they got no practical use."

Ripshin extended a tentative finger to touch his pasty and found it precisely warm enough. He picked it up and took a bite. And another. "This be good, Miz Ragna. How can I meet this dragon? Do you think he'll give me an emerald?"

"Naw. He don't give nobody nothin' without good reason. See, he cooks the pasties for Tommy and me because he's got a taste for 'em, so I make up a big batch for him every day. He don't have go out huntin' down cows for 'is dinner, and that means these Wisconsin farmers don't suspect he be here."

"The miners know." Tommy winked. "That's why they still go down in the old tunnels, lookin' for dragon gold."

"These taste like beef to me." Raphine took another bite from her pasty. "So where do you get it, Mr. Knocker?"

"Just call me Tommy. At the market, like everyone else. Sammy Robbins, what used to be a miner, runs a butcher shop. He brings me a heap of chopped beef once a week, and I give him some of Groseclose's gold. Ragna slips out in the dark of night and finds me the wild onions for the filling."

"They say true love overcomes all obstacles." Tunx eyed the pasties hungrily. "I bring you an emerald, will you marry me, Miz Raphine?"

Raphine gazed down at her plate. "Goblin law says I must marry whoever brings me an emerald first."

Ripshin turned bright red. "That'll be me, you stupid kobold. Mr. Knocker—"

"Tommy, please."

"Mr. Tommy, how can I find the dragon?"

"Easy. See them three doors on the wall down there by Tunx and Scrag?"

Ripshin nodded vigorously.

"One door goes to the catacombs where the dead go—that be the stone-cold door. One door goes to the lover's grotto, where there be an underground river. That be a warm door. One door goes to the dragon's den, and that be a nice warm door too."

"But there be four doors."

"The fourth door goes to hell. Sometimes it be warm, sometimes it be cold."

Sensing trouble, Ragna put two fingers to her mouth and whistled. One of the doors opened, and two tall blue flames emerged, taking a vaguely human form as they approached the bar. "Aha! Here be Wissa and Foss. They be bluecaps from England, and if any of us knows about marriage, it's these two."

"That be right," agreed Tommy. "They said their vows when their humans were quarrying the bluestones for Stonehenge."

Raphine had started to tremble. "Dear Ripshin, what've we gotten ourselves into? We shoulda taken that emerald ring from Henry Kay Jewelers in Chicago."

"Never fear, darlin'." Ripshin puffed out his chest. "I'll get that gem. You'll see."

"You better. I'll die before I marry a kobold."

Tunx hissed. "You and me'll go after that dragon, goblin boy. You first—go try one of those doors."

The bluecap Wissa, who seemed to be female, studied the two contestants before whispering something into Ripshin's pointy ear. The goblin listened and grinned.

Foss, the second bluecap, pointed to Tunx. "You, there, kobold, you try a door first."

Tunx looked startled. "One goes to hell, one goes to the dragon, one goes to the lover's river and one goes—I forget."

"He's not too bright," sniffed Wissa.

Tunx got off his bar stool and walked over to the set of doors, feeling each one.

Ragna whispered in Raphine's ear. "Kobolds can hear very well, but they don't have much sense of feeling. Besides, the doors keep moving. They never stay in the same place for long. You'll see."

Tunx paced back and forth, touching each door, pausing before each one."

"Get on with it," said Tommy. "We don't have an eternity to spend on this. Centuries, maybe."

Tunx pressed his palm to a door. "Here. This is it." He opened it, and a parade of foggy shapes burst out, spreading into the tavern, bringing with them a bone-chilling frost.

"Shut that door quick. You be freezing the pasties." Ragna tried shoving the door closed on the kobold, but he stuck his foot into the aperture and blocked her. For such a little creature, he possessed amazing strength. And out he came. "Must be the door to the catacombs. Those be ghosts."

"Right you are," said Tommy. "Now shoo 'em back in."

While Tunx was busy dealing with the ghosts, Ripshin stood before the doors. Tommy blinked — Ripshin vanished. "Where'd that goblin go?

Raphine smiled. "We be goblins, remember? We can swim right through stone."

Ripshin emerged, dripping. "There be a river in there — and a boat. That be where we'll go on our honeymoon, me lovely."

"My turn," snarled Tunx, who had finished disposing with the ghosts, all except for one that had bellied up to the taps and was trying to take a drink through vaporous lips. The kobold dived for another door.

In seconds Tunx popped out of his chosen door, slamming it hard behind him. "Whew!" He wiped sweat from his brow. "All the devils in hell be swarmin' after me."

Ripshin grinned. "The dragon's here. Dare you to come with me."

Tunx shoved Ripshin aside. "Me first." He pushed the door open, and hot air blasted into Tommy's tavern, taking the edge off the chill the ghosts had brought. Tunx slipped in, followed by his pal, Scrag. "Me too. I wants some dragon gold," Scrag screeched."

Ripshin disappeared and quickly reappeared. He walked to the end of the bar where his fiancée sat and dropped to his gnarly knees in front of her. In his upraised, cupped hand lay a glistening green stone the size of a goose egg. "Here be your bridal gift, me lovely. Now — will you marry me?"

"Of course, me dear. But however did you get that emerald?"

"Oh, I slipped through the rock from the river tunnel to the dragon's den. Groseclose was hungry. He said his last plate of pasties came up short."

Ragna wiped her hands on her apron. "That's not true. I fed him well."

"Maybe so, but when I pleaded for an emerald, I asked the old firebreather if he'd take a roast kobold in payment. He balked at first, so I offered him two — as long as he did the roasting."

Ragna laughed out loud. Two of the stalactites on the ceiling shattered at the sound. "That old dragon always was a romantic at heart."

"Guess Tunx and Scrag be gone for good." Tommy picked up their empty glasses and laid them in the pan of soapy water. "I 'spose that means I'll never collect on their tabs."

Ripshin stood up and took Raphine's hand. "Mister Tommy, please give us a marriage feast to remember." He reached in his pocket and pulled out a star sapphire almost as big as the emerald. "This should pay for what the kobolds drank and dinner and drinks for everyone who be still here."

Wissa and Foss stood by as witnesses as the goblins pronounced their vows. Then Tommy put an arm around Ragna's waist, being too short to reach her shoulders. "Us too," said Tommy. "It be long past time we got married."

The trolls and the knockers at the bar burst into spontaneous applause. "Past time indeed" rose the cry.

"There be room enough for four in the boat on the honeymoon river," said Ripshin. "Come along with us and we'll tour all the caves and all the tunnels under these hills."

"Yesss, yessss," hissed Wissa, her flame growing brighter. "Foss and I'll take care of the tavern while you be gone. Our weddin' gift to you."

"Mind you don't drink up all the Hubie Bock while Ragna and I be away." Tommy took off his apron, doing his best to sweep Ragna into his short arms as two of the knockers tuned up their fiddles. "And now let's dance to 'Fire on the Mountain' and drink a toast to that good old matchmaker Groseclose."

The Lily and the Rose

It was a bright, cool spring morning, a fine day for new beginnings and high time to quit weeping over what was lost. Lily been away from the barn and Dancer far too long. She was ready to start rebuilding her life on her own terms. So today she'd decided to take a long solitary ride, just she and her horse, to explore new places and let her mind play with new possibilities.

Restrained by the crossties clipped to his halter, the glossy bay horse impatiently stamped a slender

black foreleg as Lily tightened the girth on her saddle. "Easy, old boy," she murmured to the animal as
she straightened out his bridle. Dancer — for so she
had named him when she was just sixteen and still
romantic and he was still a young and excitable
horse — was her oldest and best friend, the one creature she had always trusted and still depended on,
especially now with her brief marriage ended, crumbled into dust along with her wedding bouquet and
her high hopes.

Once outside the barn she took hold of the reins
and swung lightly into the saddle. She'd almost forgotten how good this felt. Just a slight pressure from
her leg, and Dancer moved off at a high-stepping
walk toward the woods that lined the riverbank. A
network of trails meandered along both sides of the
Des Plaines River for miles, so many that she'd
never been able to explore them all. Today she
planned to ride north into places she'd never been.

The new leaves had opened on the willows and
hawthorns and were beginning to unfold on the ma-
ples. May apples and pale trilliums carpeted the forest floor. A solitary deer looked up from its breakfast
of young grass as she passed, eyed Lily with mild
curiosity and resumed grazing. Choruses of spar-
rows chittered in the undergrowth. Overhead circled a red-tailed hawk. She imagined that all nature
was welcoming her back — and then she had to
laugh at herself — such ridiculous self-centeredness!

A long straight stretch of trail lay ahead, and she
urged Dancer into a trot. His trot was smooth and
comfortable, an easy gait that ate up miles, and she
let him run a long time, enjoying the interaction of
the horse's body with her own muscles. She'd be

sore tomorrow — she was definitely out of shape — but on this brilliant day it didn't matter.

All morning horse and rider moved forward. When the trails forked Lily chose one at random, keeping the sun more or less on her right to make sure she was still trending north. Sometimes the trail took her along the muddy riverbank, sometimes along farm meadows that bordered the woodlands. It didn't matter much to her where it went as long as she didn't meet anyone else. She hadn't much felt like talking to anyone after Kevin left, packing up furniture and music collection so he could move in with that aggressive little bitch who'd won him over with her coy flirtatiousness and wide-eyed adoration — qualities Lily never had and never would. Taylor — she even envied that shameless homewrecker her name, a twenty-first century name, not old-fashioned and out of date like "Lily." And to think she'd never even suspected trouble until the day Kevin came home and announced that he was moving out. Even now, a year later, she could hardly think about it without awakening all the old hurt and anger. With an effort she pushed those thoughts away. Today she was looking for solitude. Dancer was more than enough company.

As the sun climbed higher the terrain changed. Lost in her thoughts, Lily didn't notice when land rose up into long low hills, she didn't notice when the scrub growth of the river bottomlands gave way to an open forest of beech and oak trees, she didn't even notice when the trails disappeared entirely and Dancer chose his own way under the trees. Not until noon approached and she became aware of her hunger did she begin to look around her for some place to dismount and eat the lunch she'd packed early that morning. Then she realized that somehow she'd strayed into a place where summer had come early, where the trees were in full leaf and wild roses bloomed instead of the pallid spring flowers she'd seen early that morning. Even the sun seemed hotter.

When she and Dancer topped a low hill, she was startled to see an old stone farmhouse and a couple of run-down barns nestled in the shallow valley below, and she cast a worried eye out for people. But grass and weeds had grown up around the house and its windows had been boarded up. The paint was peeling from the window frames and the slate roof badly needed work. The whole place looked as if it had been abandoned some years back.

She urged Dancer downhill so she could take a closer look. There was no road, not even a path, leading to the front door. She continued on behind the house, where she discovered what had once been a formal garden with gravel paths and even a carved marble fountain in the Italian style, complete with cherubs, long since gone dry. But roses, red, yellow and pink, still bloomed on bushes gone straggly from lack of care, and a few tiny apples were forming on a long-untended tree.

The sense of civilized emptiness appealed to her mood. The old farm looked like a pleasant place to stop and rest. She dismounted and tethered Dancer where he could graze on the lush overgrown grass. Then she took out her lunch and sat down on a crumbling stone bench to enjoy her ham and cheese sandwich.

After her lunch she grew sleepy in the warm sun and dozed for a time. When she woke the sun was nearly overhead. She guessed it must be about noon. She didn't feel like resuming her ride quite yet, and since Dancer was still contentedly grazing, she decided to stretch her legs and take a short look around.

The old house was larger than she had first realized. She discovered that she had been mistaken earlier — there was actually a tree-lined lane that led to its front entrance. However, like the garden walks and the yard, weeds had invaded its graveled surface and several of the trees had fallen.

She tried the front door. It was tightly locked and, truth be told, she wasn't really sure she wanted to go in. Despite the bright sunshine there was an eerie feel about the place. She shivered just a little, then laughed at herself for being so silly.

Back at the crumbling fountain, she noticed a particularly beautiful bloom on one of the rose-bushes, big and full, a clear light red. She leaned over it and was enchanted by its delicate spicy scent. Tempted, she reached out to it. Without her willing it, her fingers bent the stem. It snapped. The rose was in her hand, thorns and all. A tiny spot of blood appeared on her palm where one of the thorns had scratched her.

With her penknife she shaved down the thorns and tucked the rose into a buttonhole in the front of her blouse. Its scent rose up like incense, soothing her long-troubled emotions.

And then there he stood in front of her. Startled, she gasped and took a step back, only to find the fountain blocking her retreat. Yet, oddly, she had no fear of him. He was young, maybe a little older than she, and lean and tall. His red-gold hair reflected the sun. His eyes . . . too blue to be real. How was it that she hadn't seen him before now?

"You have stolen my rose," he said. His voice was low, resonant. In an instant she decided she liked it.

"Your rose? Nobody lives here. That's obvious. This place is about to fall down. How could it possibly be your rose?"

"That is my rose." His tone permitted no argument. "You have stolen it. Furthermore, you are trespassing on my land."

She pulled the flower from her blouse and held it out to him. "Take it then. Dancer and I will leave right now. I would not have come here if I realized I were trespassing."

But as she looked around, she realized that her sense of direction, always reliable, had failed her. She didn't know which way to go. Since the sun was now directly overhead, even though it was only late April, she couldn't gauge her direction from its position. Maybe Dancer could find the way...

"Never mind," said the stranger. "Please, keep it. I'm sorry. It's only right that a pretty girl should have it. It's been so long . . . well, I'm not sure I remember how to behave in polite society anymore."

"Well, I'm hardly polite society. But thank you — I think" She slipped the rose back into her buttonhole. "Now can you tell me the way back to the river so I can find my way home?"

"Here, I'll do better than that. I'll take you there." He whistled, and from out of the tall grass emerged another horse, a horse like she had never seen. It was a mare, rather small like an Arabian, and silvery white. Its mane and tail were thick and well-brushed. Its ears were distinctly strange. There was nothing wrong with their delicate taper nor the way they were set, but they were an odd color, almost red. The saddle also seemed a bit unusual, she thought — something about its angles — but nothing she could put her finger on. A multitude of tiny silver bells adorned the bridle.

"Mount up," he said, and she sprang up on Dancer's back. Her old gelding lifted up his head and held it proudly high, and as he walked he raised his knees like the show horse he had once been.

"That's a beautiful animal," he commented, and Dancer stepped even higher. She began to feel attracted to this peculiar young man.

They rode in silence. She had a thousand questions about the old farm that she wanted to ask him, but this didn't seem to be the time.

At length they reached a small clear stream. She did not remember having crossed it before. Beyond it the trees grew smaller, thinner, less green. He turned his horse to the right and rode along the stream for a short way, until he came to an arched stone bridge.

"Lily," he said. "Lily Cameron."

"What? How did you know my name? I never told you."

"Never mind. My name is Tom Linn. Did you know that people used to think knowing someone's name gave one power over that person? Well, in my world, it's true. I'm giving you that power. Lily, when you want to see me again, ride to this bridge and call out my name. I'll come to you."

"How — ?" she began again.

"The river is just over that little rise. When you see it, turn left. You'll be on your way home. When you want to come back, just say my name to Dancer and he'll bring you here. Remember that. You will remember, won't you?"

She was about to say something ridiculous, like "I don't know when I'll have a free minute," or, "I'll be washing my hair every night for the next three months," or, worse, "This is all very weird and I'll do no such thing." But when she actually spoke she said, "Yes, I'll remember."

His eyes flashed a brief, almost tentative smile as he turned his horse and urged it into an easy canter back toward the old house. Dancer shook his head and stepped into a brisk walk, carrying her away from this uncanny land where it was already summer.

During the ride back to the barn she replayed the encounter over and over again, trying to understand what exactly had happened and why she felt strangely excited, as though lifted out of her own everyday world. But by the time she had rubbed Dancer down and returned him to his stall, the concerns of her daily existence had already shoved their unruly way into her brain. The difficult drive back to the city on an expressway packed with overtired weekend travelers dulled her recollections further. By Monday night, after a day of trying to write brilliant ad copy for clients she didn't think appreciated it, the event had taken on the ghostly colors of a dream. Only the perfumed rose nestled in a tiny vase on her dresser remained to remind her that something very much out of the ordinary had indeed occurred.

The next weekend brought on a spring downpour. It was too wet to ride outdoors, so she put Dancer through his paces in the indoor arena. Another week passed without event, except that Kevin showed up on Thursday night unannounced and demanded that she produce his set of Mahler symphony recordings. She didn't like Mahler and she didn't know where the old CDs were, though in some perverse way she still would have liked to please him. But he was much more interested in Mahler than in her, and when he left scowling she allowed herself to cry just a little. Once she had loved Kevin, and she still felt the sting of his rejection.

On Friday night she had a date with one of the senior media buyers from her agency. Ryan O'Malley was nice-looking and attentive. He escorted her to the Italian Village for dinner and then to a movie and finally to the Red Lion pub for a nightcap. When he took her home shortly after midnight, he asked no more from her than a good-night kiss. It was okay. She agreed to join him the next afternoon for some gallery-hopping.

That night she didn't sleep well. Maybe it was the heavy Italian dinner she'd eaten or the whisky sours she'd downed at the pub. She dreamed of a place where it was already summer, of a run-down stone house and a garden gone to seed, of a young man with eyes more blue than any she'd ever seen. She dreamed of Kevin and that self-centered Taylor, his new lady love. She finally decided that getting up tired was better than revisiting her troubled dreams.

When she got out of bed the first thing she saw was the rose. She remembered that she hadn't watered it for several days, and in fact the vase was dry. But the rose was as fresh, as soft and as fragrant as it had been on the day she'd plucked it.

On an impulse so abrupt it startled her, she called Ryan and postponed their afternoon date, pleading a headache. Maybe next Saturday, she said. He seemed disappointed.

"Can we do it Friday then?" she asked. "That's when all the gallery openings happen. Or how about lunch on Tuesday?" She didn't know why she encouraged him, except that she was lonely, and Tom Linn seemed worlds distant when she was back in the city. Ryan said he'd call her back about it later, and she didn't press it.

She dressed in her best riding clothes. She was not the kind of woman who made men turn around on the street. But she thought she wasn't bad looking, with her tapered oval face, large gray eyes and clear skin. And her figure was at least okay, if not spectacular. The close-fitting riding jodhpurs flattered her slender waist and long legs. She fastened her reddish brown hair into a neat single braid so it wouldn't blow into her face when she rode. Then she made a couple of sandwiches and drove out to the stable.

Dancer seemed to know something was up. The tall bay horse stood with unusual patience while she groomed him, and he let her tighten his girth on the first try, instead of taking a deep breath and making his belly swell up as he usually did.

Outside the barn she mounted Dancer and then held him still for a moment. The warm sun gave her courage. "This is absolutely stupid," she said out loud. "I dreamed all that nonsense. Okay. Well." She took a deep breath. "Dancer, please find Tom Linn."

He turned his head to the side to gaze at her out of one soft brown eye, then looked ahead as she gathered the reins loosely into her hands. He snorted and stepped forward into that steady ground-eating walk he had. About a mile onto the trail, with no urging from her, he shifted to a trot. She had absolutely no idea which way to go, since the last time she had taken this ride she had chosen trails at random. She knew only that they had to ride north. So she let Dancer have his head and merely tried to establish landmarks in her own mind as the old gelding turned first this way, then that, now walking, now trotting as he pleased.

Again it was nearing noon when the feel of the land changed and low hills began to lift them out of the bottomlands along the river. Still she was surprised when Dancer snorted, slowed to a walk and then stopped. Since it was later into the spring, the transition between new growth and the trees of full summer was less marked than it had been two weeks ago, but there was clearly a difference, some kind of border here. And there, just coming into view, was the stone bridge and the stream where she had last seen the mysterious Tom Linn.

Dancer refused to cross the bridge. She urged him forward, but he merely circled this way and that and would not obey the pressure of her knees.

"There's nothing to be afraid of, sweetie," she said. "Here, you can follow me." She dismounted and walked toward the bridge, holding on to his bridle as she led him. She set one foot on the bridge herself and knew at once that she must not cross, not alone. Something sinister awaited there. But so did Tom Linn and to see him again seemed the most important thing she would ever do.

"Dummy! I knew none of this really happened," she said to herself. "I must have dreamed it. No. The bridge is here. Dancer did find the right place. Now I'm supposed to call out his name. Tom! Tom Linn!"

She heard a sound of bells, a silvery chiming. Dancer whinnied and from somewhere nearby a horse answered him. And then there was the man sitting straight on his white horse, the sunlight burnishing his fine cheekbones and making his red-gold hair gleam. He was smiling, dismounting, reaching out his hand to her. She took it and was across the bridge in an instant, through whatever barrier had blocked her passage. Dancer followed of his own accord.

Behind her it was still early spring. Here it was high summer, as she had remembered it, a summer where the colors of the flowers and even the grass were more intense than any she had ever seen, a summer where the sun gave more light than it should. It reminded her of stories her Scottish grandmother had told of mysterious lands that somehow touched those of mortal men, yet were not of their world. Her grandfather and even her father pooh-poohed those stories, calling them tales for children, but she knew her grandmother had believed them true. And if there was any chance that her grandmother might be right, then she had crossed one of those boundaries between worlds and had stepped into something beyond her understanding.

But this man, this Tom Linn, he seemed normal enough, except that the clothes he wore were a little odd, not blue jeans and a colorful sport shirt but close-fitting trousers and a plain shirt, both made of a finely woven brown cloth that resembled cotton but wasn't. And there was the matter of his horse with its odd red ears and its bridle hung with tiny bells, the like of which had never been seen at any barn or horse show she knew of.

"I'm so glad you came," said Tom. "I don't think many women would have been trusting enough to follow my instructions and return here."

"Foolish may be the better word," Lily said. "There's something not quite right here. Well, that's understating it. This isn't real. It can't be. On one side of a bridge there's a world I know, where it's spring and that's what the calendar says it should be. It can't be summer yet — and here it is. And on some impulse I don't understand I've ridden out to see a man I've met once and only briefly, a man who seems to live in this peculiar place. And only my horse can find him. For all I know, you're an axe murderer and I'll never be heard from again."

"No, this is not exactly your world — not our world. I should say. And I'm not an axe murderer. However, I'm in the peculiar position of not being able to cross that bridge. You could say I'm a prisoner. But not a convict. And by daylight there's nothing here that can harm you. Let's not talk about that now — it's something to discuss later, when we know each other. Today let's just take a ride and enjoy the sunshine and get acquainted."

She'd already heard more in that brief speech than she dared to analyze. If she thought about what he'd said, she could become very frightened. So she nodded and swung back up on Dancer. Tom mounted his silvery mare and led the way. They passed the old farmhouse.

"Do you know who used to live there?" Lily asked. "I wonder what became of them."

"This land belongs to me," said Tom. "Once my parents, my brother and I lived here. But my brother was killed in Viet Nam. My parents died a little later. But that was years ago. By then I'd vanished from their world, and they thought I was also dead. But as you can see, I wasn't. I was just out of reach, through no cause of my own choosing. Now they're gone too. I hope someday that I can fix up this old place — but I've said too much. Tell me about yourself."

His smile dazzled her. This was the moment where she usually froze up, intimidated by a good-looking male who, she thought, wasn't really interested in a rather plain girl like her. And he was a very attractive man. But there was something about him — she felt as though she could confide her deepest secrets to him and they would be safe.

"I grew up on a place something like this," she began. "In Kentucky, near Lexington. That's horse country, so I learned to ride young. My dad was an engineer and my mother was a teacher. But my grandparents were from the Cumberland Mountains — old Scots-Irish stock. If it weren't for my grandmother, I don't think I would have come here

today. She believed . . . she believed in things that
nobody could explain. Like this place. Like you being here. Like me finding you."

"There are more things in heaven and earth,
Horatio, than are dreamt of in your philosophy." He
laughed. "I'm sorry, everyone quotes that at the first
sign of anything extraordinary. But it's true."

"Hamlet, of course," Lily said. "It's one of my favorite Shakespeare plays. I was an English major...
Anyway, by the time I was old enough to be thinking about college, I was all too eager to leave home
and try my wings in a really big city like Chicago. I
don't know if it was such a great decision. I met my
husband in my senior year — "

"You didn't mention a husband!" Tom stiffened
in the saddle.

"I don't have one anymore," she said. "Kevin
found somebody else he liked better. Besides that
was awhile ago." She rattled on, talking about her
job, her horse, her Mom and Dad back in Lexington,
her married sisters, her nephews and nieces. It
wasn't like her to talk so much and so freely, but she
was afraid that if she stopped talking, he might tell
her more than she wanted to know about this place.
About his situation. Luckily he didn't seem bored
with her prattle. In fact, he seemed to be hanging on
her every word.

As they rode the land grew rockier and the hills
steeper. After what seemed a very short time she
heard the sound of falling water. He guided her into
a steep ravine, where they encountered a clear rushing stream. "This creek leads to the one you crossed
to enter here," said Tom. "There's a very nice little

waterfall just ahead. I thought we could stop and have lunch there."

"I brought some sandwiches for us," she said.

He looked at her and smiled. "That was thoughtful of you. I brought a few things too. We'll be well-fed."

A sudden thought struck her and she gasped involuntarily. "I can't eat your food! If I do, I'll never be able to leave here. My grandmother told me — " She felt herself turning red. This was superstition talking — her grandmother's fairy tales awakening in her. She was suddenly ashamed and fell silent.

He laughed. "Lily, some things in the old tales are true, and some are just imaginings on the part of folk who really didn't know why certain people disappeared for good when the Fair Folk were about. Believe me, it wasn't the food.

"The fairies — or the elves — call them whatever you want — have their own reasons for capturing mortals. They will steal babies away because so few are born among them. They will take gifted musicians because they love all music and want to listen to skillful singers and players. And they will seize mortal men and women they find handsome because they want the novelty of lovers who are similar to themselves yet very different.

"They usually permit musicians to go back home. They seldom give back the babies, and they almost never allow their mortal lovers to return. But fairy food has nothing to do with it. You can eat it without fear."

They entered a meadow surrounded by low rocky banks. At the farther end of the little glen, the creek fell in a slender double stream from the rocks into a small pool.

Tom dismounted and looped his mare's reins loosely upon his saddle so she could lower her head and graze.

"You're saying this really is fairyland, aren't you?" Lily said, not quite believing.

"What do you think?" he asked gently as he held Dancer's bridle so she could dismount.

"I don't know. I mean — this is crazy. But I know this place isn't like anywhere I've ever seen or ever been. It's like it's not real."

"Oh, it's real enough. But you're right. It's not like the world you see every day. This place exists alongside your reality. In some places it touches your world, and in a few places you can even cross over into it. Your Scottish grandmother would have called this place Faerie" — he pronounced it *Fy-er-ee-a* "and she would have told you stories about the dangerous enchantments of the Fair Folk. There are no cute little Tinker Bells here. The Fair Folk are tall, proud, beautiful and —" he hesitated a moment — "Well, they're not truly heartless, but they do not think and respond as we do, even though I think that we mortals and those immortals are somehow related."

"But you're not —" What could she say? You're not a fairy? Damn right — he sure didn't appear to be gay. What about an elf? Don't they wear brown and carry bows? Tom was wearing brown, but he didn't seem to have a bow. Well, what, then?

"No, I'm not. I'm just a human being like you are, one of the captured ones. I must stay in their world, at least most of the time. But because this land, my land, was part of the mortal world, it isn't fully a part of Faerie, even though the touch of their enchantment affects it. It allows me to come here, yet you can enter it, and you did because I called you. I dreamed of you, and I called you before you came here the first time. Didn't you wonder how I knew your name?"

"Yes, of course. But I was so startled I didn't know what to do. And everything was so strange that day."

"I had dreamed it. As I dreamed of your horse and used him to deliver you here. Now bring on your sandwiches — I haven't had a ham sandwich in years, and it will be a real treat. I hope you'll enjoy some of the things I've brought. I promise you, eating my food is perfectly safe."

Tom began unpacking his saddlebags, laying the contents out on a flat rock. There was a tall glass bottle that held a straw-colored wine. There were sliced meats on translucent porcelain plates, a salad made up of unfamiliar greens, an assortment of red, blue and purple berries, little cakes with sugared blossoms decorating them. Just looking at the meal he'd set out made her hungry.

"We probably won't even need these sandwiches," Lily said, opening up her small sack and pulling them out anyway.

"What's that — ham sandwiches and a chocolate bar too? Bittersweet? Oh, sheer joy!" he said. "How I've missed chocolate! The Fair Folk simply don't have it."

"There are two bars," she said. "They're all yours. I can always get more."

They ate. The foods he had brought tasted like the proverbial morsels for the gods. Yet he seemed to relish the simple everyday sandwiches she'd packed in more than the delicacies of the fairy realm. Then they lay back in the grass and watched the clouds float by overhead. She felt like she had known him forever — and not at all. It was an un-settling sensation.

It's getting late," Tom finally said. "You should go back. As much as I want you to stay here, it would not do for you to be here when night falls. That's when the Fair Folk ride."

Once more he escorted her to the bridge. For an all-too-brief moment, he embraced her, and his lips brushed her hair lightly.

"Lily. You will come back? Tomorrow?"

"I'll come back tomorrow," she promised, "but after that it won't be until next weekend. I have to work."

The next morning Lily was at the barn early, carrying several chocolate bars for Tom and carrots for Dancer and Tom's mare, Paloma. When he saw her Dancer neighed eagerly, as if he knew where they were going. The old gelding was as lively as if he'd dropped half a dozen years or more. Soon they were at the stone bridge. Tom did not fail her. When she called to him, there he was.

"Would you like to see the old farm today?" he asked her.

She would. And so they rode through orchards of gnarled cherry and apple trees, through flower-starred meadows bordered with white fencing like the horse farms of Lexington, along the ragged edges of untended woodlots and through fallow fields where stray cornstalks and soybean shoots poked up through the weeds that had taken over.

"This must have been a beautiful farm once," she remarked.

"It was. Maybe it will be again. I guess it's up to me if it's up to anybody."

"Well then, why don't you start?"

"Ah. You see, I can't, not while this land is un-free. It's imprisoned as much as I am. As it is, it's only my memories of its past and my own family that keep it from fading away entirely."

He didn't volunteer any more information, and she thought it wiser not to probe too deeply yet.

Losing herself in the magic of this strange land and Tom's presence, Lily had little sense of time passing until once more Tom was escorting her to the bridge. And then it was back to work on Monday morning.

Surrounded by concrete towers and facing the stresses of her job, Lily once again felt the magic of Tom Linn slipping away from her. No matter how hard she tried to recapture the enchantment of the weekend, the unforgiving realities of her weekday world drove it away. She knew she could go back — but when she was arguing a point in a client meeting or struggling over a line of copy on the computer screen, it just didn't seem relevant.

On Wednesday she ran into Ryan in the employee cafeteria.

"Are we still on for Friday?" he asked. "The galleries?"

Lily had decided she liked his attentions. His Irish red hair and blue eyes reminded her of Tom, though not the freckles. He had an engaging grin, and while his ears stuck out just a little too far from his head, it wasn't a serious flaw. He laughed easily. And his prospects were stellar. Already he managed a staff of six assistant media buyers. His salary was good and moving up. He wore suits she could understand, not odd brown trousers and shirts with laces instead of buttons.

So she said yes.

During the next two days she concentrated hard on her assignments, keeping thoughts of Tom at bay. The result was some unusually good copy. Her boss was pleased. There was talk of a raise.

On Friday at five she met Ryan in the lobby of the building where they worked. They walked over to the River North gallery district, bucking the crowds headed single-mindedly to the commuter train stations.

"Let's see how many openings we can hit before they run out of food and wine," suggested Ryan, winking.

Now there's a true art lover. She kept that rather snide thought to herself.

It wasn't easy, with Ryan so determined to drink his way through River North, but she did manage to hold him back long enough to actually look at some of the artworks on display. One watercolor caught her eye. A landscape, it looked very much like the spot in the woods where she had been meeting Tom. Even the arched stone bridge was there. It wasn't part of the featured exhibition. It didn't seem to be signed, though perhaps the frame concealed the artist's name. But there was a price tag on it: $300.

Perhaps the cost wasn't high compared to many of the works on sale in the gallery, but $300 was still a strain on Lily's budget. Just the same she soon found herself writing out a check to the gallery owner. The painting was wrapped and tucked under her arm before she even had time to realize what she'd done.

When the galleries closed down, Tom took her out to dinner. Then he wanted to see a movie. When she finally got home, it was almost 2 a.m. She unwrapped the painting and put it on top of her dresser, leaning it against the wall. It looked right propped up near the rose in its vase.

Lily was tired and feeling the effects of too much wine, so she climbed into bed without setting an alarm. And she awoke promptly at 6:30. The sun was already up and her head ached. She rolled over and tried to go back to sleep. Outside her apartment window, a robin was lustily whistling. "Oh, shut up," she said to the bird, who paid her no attention at all. Somewhere a horse whinnied. Probably a carriage horse going back to the barn after a night of hauling tourists up and down Michigan Avenue. The breeze smelled of roses. Roses again.

She sat up in bed. On her dresser Tom's rose glowed in the early morning sun. She looked at her new painting, the trees, the bridge. Was that a figure emerging from the brush on the far side of the stream? She got up and looked more closely. Maybe it was a trick of the light. She couldn't be sure. But in the sunlight she could make out the signature, which had been rather carefully worked into the blades of grass in one corner: Linn. And a date: 1933.

She gave up any idea of sleep and took two aspirin and a shower. Within the hour she had donned
her riding clothes and headed for the barn and Tom.
As always when she was in his world the hours flew
by. Too soon Tom had taken her back to the stone
bridge. Just before they said good-bye, Tom took
something from the small leather pouch that hung
from his belt and held it out to her: A tiny, perfectly
formed golden rose, suspended from a fine golden
chain.

"I can't accept that," Lily protested. "It's too
good."

"Why? Don't you think you know me well
enough?"

"Well, no, not exactly. But that's the kind of
thing a man gives a woman when he's — " She realized what she was about to say and quickly clipped
her sentence off.

"When he's in love with her? You're quite right.
Please accept it, Lily. It was my mother's once."

She let him fasten the clasp at the back of her
neck. He had to come very close to do that. When he
was done, he put both hands on her shoulders and
carefully turned her around to face him. Then he
kissed her softly and rather solemnly before he left
her at the bridge.

Back at work on Monday, she knew something
in her had changed. The city could no longer distract
her from Tom. If anything, the world she shared
with him on weekends had become far more real
than the one in which she lived and worked. She
went through the work week as though she were
sleepwalking. Her boss was no longer pleased.

She had promised Ryan she'd join him for dinner on Friday, and there was no escaping it. But it wasn't going to be a pleasant evening.

They made small talk through the meal. That was the problem, Lily thought. I don't have anything in common with this person. He'll make a great husband for someone but not for me. Why did I even think he could be good for me? He's never been near a horse, doesn't even like the country, and has no real interest in art. He doesn't read anything but business books and The Wall Street Journal. Why did I let it go this far?

So after they'd eaten their calamari and their pasta and were sipping Frangelico from tiny glasses, she took a deep breath. "Ryan, I don't really know a nice way to say this, but I think it would be better for both of us to stop seeing each other."

Ryan abruptly swallowed more Frangelico than he should have and went into a fit of coughing.

"Wait a minute," he said when he could talk again. "I don't think I understand this. I like you, and I know you like me."

"That's true," Lily replied. "I do like you. That's why this is hard. But Ryan, there's someone else I care for very much. It's just not fair for me to keep leading you on until I'm sure where I'm going in this other relationship."

"You don't have to decide yet. I'll understand," he said, almost pleading.

It hurt. He was starting to care for her. She could see it. But she was falling in love with the strange man of the woods and the river, the man who rode a white horse with red ears and who talked of fairies as though he spoke with them daily. And she believed he did.

She couldn't tell Ryan any of this.

"There are lots of girls right here in the agency who are prettier and more interesting than I am," she told him, "and I know that most of them would be pleased to be seen with you."

"Don't sell yourself short, Lily. Any man with eyes to see knows you're one of the most beautiful flowers of all womankind."

"Sure and you've kissed the Blarney Stone," Lily said in her best Irish brogue, trying to lift the mood a bit. "Ryan, I've been hurt plenty in my relationships with men, and I don't want to make someone else feel as bad as I've felt. If we go on, I'll hurt you. I know it."

"Can't we still be — never mind, that's a really dumb thing to say." He picked up the check and stood to go. "C'mon, I'll take you home."

When he dropped her off he kissed her lightly and held her hand for a moment. "See ya, Lily. It's been fun. Let me know if you change your mind."

And he was gone.

The golden rose on its slender chain lay warm against the pulse in her throat.

The next morning and every weekend after that she rode Dancer to find Tom Linn. She had discovered she could talk to Tom about anything, without any fear, embarrassment or shame. He listened, made no judgments, sometimes gave her good advice. Sometimes he talked about himself, how he had gone to school at the University of Wisconsin at Madison where they had a fine agricultural program, so he could come home and help his father with the orchards and the horses — especially the horses. His family had raised fine riding and draft horses, fiery Arabians and elegant Saddlebreds and placid, tawny Belgian draft horses. She had never known such a comfortable relationship with any man, nor such happiness. Somewhere deep in her heart she knew that it couldn't last, that in spite of the sunshine something dark waited to spoil her happiness, but whenever that fear threatened to surface, she pushed it away.

One Saturday morning in mid-May she set off as usual full of joyful anticipation. But a little more than halfway there, or so she judged, Dancer fell out of his canter and began to favor his right leg.

"What's wrong, sweetie?" she murmured to her horse as she dismounted, fearing what she might find. She lifted his slender leg, rested his hoof on her thigh. He'd thrown his shoe. That might not have been so bad, but part of the hoof wall had been torn. No wonder he was limping.

"Now what?" she asked the woods around her, as though the trees could hear. "It's a long way to the bridge. It's even farther to the barn. Dancer, sweetie, what should we do?"

He nuzzled her shoulder as if to tell her, "Well, if you don't know, I'm sure I can't say."

Later it occurred to her that it would have been wiser — very much wiser — to have gone back to the barn. But she wanted so very badly to see Tom. She had an old jacket, one she usually kept in her saddlebags in case the day turned unexpectedly cold or wet. She took it out and tore off a generous section of the back, wrapping it around the injured hoof and tying it on with a short piece of rope. Then she led Dancer forward.

In spite of all her attempts to memorize landmarks, she still felt she was guessing at direction. Then she realized that her poor lame horse was still guiding her, balking when she tried to lead him down the wrong trail and following eagerly when she chose the correct fork.

"So you want to see him as much as I do," she said to herself as much as the animal. "What does that mean, I wonder? What have we got ourselves into, old friend?"

She had not realized how long it would take her to walk to the stone bridge. When she finally did arrive, it was already around three in the afternoon and Tom was there. It seemed to her that his face with tense with concern for her.

"Lily, thank God!" he said. "Come across the bridge, quickly! I can't keep this gate open even a minute longer. What happened? What's wrong?"

"It's Dancer," she said, turning her face away from him so he wouldn't see the tears of weariness and relief she was trying to hold back. "He threw a shoe and he's lame."

He took her face in his hands so she couldn't look away. "You're pretty worried, aren't you? And tired too. This must have happened quite a ways back. That's okay, you can cry. It doesn't frighten me."

And in spite of herself, she settled into his arms, weeping quietly against his shoulder, grateful for his strength and his caring. She'd had very little of either with Kevin.

"I may be able to help Dancer," he said "My mare can carry us both — climb on up behind me, and we'll see what we can do about Dancer's hoof."

They went straight to the run-down barns behind the house. Tom unsaddled his mare and turned her out into the paddock, then asked Lily to follow as he led Dancer into the nearer of the two old structures.

"There's an old forge in here, and I know a little about shoeing horses." Tom tugged hard on the door, and it opened with a reluctant creak. "Phew! It's pretty musty. I doubt if anyone's been in here since my Mom and Dad died. Let's see if we can get some windows open, and maybe the overhead light will work —" He reached for the string, and the light came on, revealing an array of blacksmithing tools hanging on the planked walls. There were also an anvil and a small forge. He pulled down an old leather apron. "This thing is pretty stiff, but I guess it will do. Let's get Dancer in the crossties and have a look."

He lifted the injured hoof with a relaxed ease that suggested real skill and probed at it with a hoof pick. "It's not as bad as you might have thought, Lily. The hoof's not split. We're going to have to trim it some, and his other forefoot to match, but with a little rest he'll be just fine. I'll see if I can get this old forge working so we can shape some new shoes for him."

She watched as he cut away part of the hoof wall with a nipper and then rasped down the base of the hoof itself. Next he pulled the shoe off the other front hoof and shaped the hoof to match the injured one. Digging out a new set of shoes from an old wooden crate, he put them into the fire to soften them. Then he applied them to Dancer's hooves and hammered them until they fit the horse as closely and exactly as possible. Finally Tom tapped the nails that secured the shoes in place and released Dancer from the ties.

The big gelding took a few careful steps, still favoring the hoof that had been injured. Then he seemed to realize he could walk without pain. Tom led him out into the paddock where Paloma was already grazing and turned him loose. He pranced a little and settled down to sample the grass.

"He'll be fine tomorrow if you take it easy with him," Tom told Lily. "You do understand that there's no way you can get back any more today, don't you? For one thing, it's long past the hour when the gates between our two worlds can be opened. For another, even assuming I could get you out, I don't think you could walk back to the barn before dark. But we must get you indoors, so there is no chance that any of the Fair Folk will find you on this land. If that happens, you'll be in grave danger. Let's go to the house."

"Can you get in?" she said. "I tried the door when I first found this place. It seemed to be locked pretty tight."

"Only against strangers — people who shouldn't be here — not against me. I come here often, to remember," he said. And he simply turned the doorknob and opened the front door.

A soft coolness welcomed them. Stepping onto a floor of gray slate tiles, Lily saw a large open room a few steps lower, carpeted in pale greys and ivories, and other rooms all at different levels that seemed to flow from and into the main room. She and Tom went first into the big room, which must have been the living room, for large upholstered sofas and chairs were arranged in a conversational grouping beside a large stone fireplace. Plain wooden tables of varying heights and sizes were scattered throughout. There was an old television set with a small gray screen. The style of the furniture, Lily saw, was vaguely Southwestern, rather timeless, but the television set was a type that had been manufactured in the 1970s. Lily knew that because her family had once had one like it.

"Tom," she ventured, "How much time has passed since you were taken away from here? How old are you really?"

He led her into the big open kitchen. It had more cabinet space than it seemed anyone could ever need and the most modern appliances the 1970s had to offer.

"First, let's see if there's any coffee in here — oh, good, here's a can that's never been opened." He brewed a potful and took it over to the big oak table. He took two mugs down from a cabinet and wiped them off.

"Sit down," he said, and then pulled up a chair so that he could face her and take her hands. "This will not be easy to explain. I am only a year or two older than you are, although it is difficult to be sure. Here comes the hard part. I was born in 1945."

Lily felt her jaw drop.

"I was born in 1945, and I was taken into Faerie when I was 25. But time doesn't flow the same way in Faerie as it does in the other world. I have been in Faerie only a couple of years in their terms, and so I have aged very little. However, twenty-five or more years have passed in the world outside — your world. So you probably weren't even born when I was captured, but now we are almost the same age.

"My father died in 1975, after both his sons had been lost to him, and my mother died not long afterward. I know the dates because I was sometimes allowed to visit here, though only at night when everyone was sleeping, and I would read the dates on the newspapers that had been thrown into the trash. I think they both died of broken hearts because they really weren't very old. They just didn't have enough left to live for."

Tears welled up in her eyes for them and for him.

"Don't cry, Lily. Death is not as final as it may seem. As for my exile, there may be a way to end it. Come on, let me show you the rest of the house."

It was much bigger than it looked from the outside. She supposed that, like so much in this strange, magically touched region, that some charm or enchantment made it appear to be something that it was not. But which was real — the outside or the inside?

There were fine paintings and drawings from the thirties, forties and fifties on the walls — and several watercolors signed "Linn." "Those are my mother's," Tom said. "She loved to paint this farm."

"I have one of her paintings," Lily blurted out. "I found it at a gallery a few weeks ago. It shows the bridge — and sometimes in certain lights I think I see a man in it too, half-concealed in the brush."

Tom looked at her oddly. "She used to be represented by a gallery in the city," he said. "But that was obviously many years ago. I don't remember a painting like that."

"There was a morning when it made me come to you."

"That sounds like my Mom," he said. "Still looking out for me."

"It's very strange," said Lily.

"Maybe we aren't meant to understand some things," Tom replied.

Lily saw sculptures of marble and bronze placed as casually as ashtrays on shelves and tables. Expansive library shelves were piled with books on many subjects.

There was no dust to be seen anywhere.

She thought they had seen everything when Tom opened one last door.

"This was my room once," he said. Bookshelves lined the walls. A steel-stringed acoustic guitar rested in a stand in one corner. There were flute-like recorders in several sizes on a table nearby, along with books of music. The stereo system had a turn-table, a tape deck and a tuner but no CD player. There was a big roll-top desk, a couple of comfortable upholstered chairs and a large bed covered with a patchwork quilt that reminded her of the ones her grandmother made. A large bay window looked out into the old garden — she could see the fountain, the apple tree and the rosebush whose flower had called Tom to her.

He stood in the middle of the room looking somehow lonely and lost. She said simply, "Oh, Tom," and impulsively wrapped her arms around him in a hug. He stiffened for a second, then relaxed and began stroking her hair. She felt his hands on her braid, loosening the strands and brushing out her long hair with gentle fingers.

She suddenly became very aware of his body's warmth, of the powerful muscles of his arms and chest under the soft fabric of his shirt. She turned her face up to his and met his lips with hers. She knew there could be danger here — when was the last time she had made love to a man? — but she no longer cared.

She let her hands slide down from his shoulders to his wrists. Unlacing his cuffs, she gripped his wrists lightly and then moved up to his powerful forearms. Her fingertips told her about the smoothness of the skin inside his wrists, the crisp hairs on his arms, the wiry muscles and tendons. From there her hands ventured to his biceps and then on to the well-muscled shoulders. Her hands craved his chest . . . that would be another unlacing job. She heard him gasp when her hand stroked his bare breast.

Not that his hands had been idle. Her nipples had hardened under his touch and she felt her breasts were so hot and swollen that they could have burst open the straining fabric of her shirt. As the heat spread to her groin, she simply gave up any idea of self-control. She cried out, a little mewing cry of fear, hope and desire.

At her cry, Tom's hands stopped moving on her body. "Am I hurting you?"

She couldn't help but giggle. "No, no, no. No! We shouldn't be doing this, should we?"

"Who said? You and I have been leading up to this for a long time. Don't you know by now that I love you?"

They all say that, she thought. That's what Kevin said. I guess he thought he loved me, for awhile. But this is true. I know it is. I think it is. Do I care? Not now!

She slipped his shirt off. He was so beautiful, so lean, so powerfully muscled — so naked. She had thought he would be beautiful; she'd seen it in the easy way he moved, the confident way he handled himself. But actually seeing his bare body made it so much better.

Somehow they both escaped all their clothes and stood with their bodies pressed hard together. Then he stepped back and simply looked at her for a long moment.

"Lily, you are my rose, my rose indeed," he said. Then he picked her up and laid her on the bed. He eased himself on top of her, supporting himself on his elbows and knees, and she opened her legs to receive him.

He was in no hurry. Neither was she. She'd never known anything like this, never desired a man in this way. She wanted this joy, this heat, to last forever.

Of course it didn't.

She wept a little afterward. He held her close, stroking her hair. "This is only the first of many times we'll share this pleasure," Tom said to her, "and it's only one of the many kinds of pleasure we'll share together."

They slept a little while and made love again. Then the sun went down and they heard the nighthawks keening as they began their nightly flights just outside their window. Tom got up and pulled down the window shades.

"Lily, I can't stay with you through the night," Tom told her. "I'm expected to ride with the Fair Folk and their Queen. If I don't go they may suspect something. I'll be back at dawn. Until then I want you to wait here. It will be safe. And you have the run of the house."

What choice did she have? "I won't be afraid," she said.

The water system in the house seemed intact, but there was no hot water. Tom washed up in cold water, saying that he was used to it. "I'll get the old hot water heater started for you," he said, "and bring you food."

Too soon he was at the door, opening it into the dark. "Stay out of sight," he warned her after their final kiss. He went out into the night.

The house was too empty without him, so after she'd soaked in a hot bath, she retreated to his old room. For awhile she sat up and looked at one of his books, but reading was a lost cause. She could do nothing but think about him. Faintly she heard bells but then thought she'd just imagined them. There were other odd noises outside the house, scratchings and whimperings and hootings. Small animals, owls perhaps? After all of Tom's warnings she dared not look out the window. Finally exhaustion caught up with her, and she climbed back into the bed they had shared. She fell asleep right away and dreamed that he was stroking her arms, her breasts, her belly — and she woke to find the window shades open to pale daylight and him sitting beside her on the bed.

"Darling girl, I've had a look at Dancer's hoof already," he was saying. "You can ride him back today. But we have lots of time before you have to go."

And it started all over again.

By early June Lily knew she had conceived a child by Tom Linn. By a man who was somehow trapped in a supernatural world where she could not stay.

But it was his baby, and no matter what, she wanted it.

When she finally told him she was pregnant, he seemed elated — and worried. "Soon, Lily, very soon, a crux is coming. I've just found out that on Midsummer Eve, my fate will be decided. Either I will be doomed to remain in Faerie forever, or I will be rescued. I don't know which it will be. What will you do with a baby if I am forever lost to you?"

"I will cherish it because it is yours," Lily said. She wanted to add, that is, if I can live without you, but she bit her tongue and left those words unsaid.

"You are the key to our happiness, my little flower. Only someone who loves me can save me, and it must be someone who is brave beyond belief. On Midsummer Eve, the Queen of Faerie and her people will leave this region for a time — a short time for them, an infinity of years for you and me. I must go with them, and I will be lost to you and our child unless you can face terrors that you cannot even dream of — and I will be the worst terror you must face."

"Tell me what I must do and I will do it," she said, trying to sound much braver than she felt.

"Dearest Lily, remember that I am your baby's father. Remember that I love you no matter what happens. And then remember what I am about to tell you, engrave it on your heart and pray for us."

It was only two weeks until midsummer. Lily quit her job abruptly, with only a week's notice. Her boss seemed relieved. She hadn't been concentrating on her work for weeks now, and she figured he was about to fire her anyway. Just the same she did her best to get everything in order so that her successor, whoever that might be, could easily pick up where she'd left off. It just wasn't in her to walk away from the place and leave a mess behind.

The last week before Midsummer Eve, she went daily to the old farm to be with Tom. And then finally came the day, as inevitable and unstoppable as a big truck with no brakes rolling down a mountain side, the day that would end in either their lifelong happiness or her eternal despair.

Tom had not permitted her to come to his farm that day, warning her that the Queen of Faerie would sense her presence on enchanted land. "You must be at the stone bridge by midnight," he had instructed her. "There's no other way."

Before she left home late that afternoon she took Tom's rose from its vase. It was still fresh and sweet, as tender and fragrant as the day she had plucked it. She pinned it to the lapel of her riding jacket and set out for the barn. Once there she exercised Dancer lightly to loosen him up and then washed and groomed him until his coat gleamed. She even applied polish to his hooves, partly to help keep her mind off what was to come and partly so he'd make a fair showing even against the horses of Faerie — whatever good that would do her. Gradually the other riders finished their chores, and by nine or so everyone, even the grooms, were gone. It was time. She saddled up Dancer and slipped out of a side door, leading him until they were well away from the buildings.

The final glow of the sunset was fading when at last she mounted and set out. She was grateful that a full moon was rising, giving off a fair amount of light. And Dancer knew the way, she reminded herself.

But after she had been riding an hour or so, clouds began scudding across the stars and obscuring the moon. Horses don't see well at night, she knew, and she surely didn't either, not in the dark of the woods. Dancer kept striding forward, but she no longer felt confident that he could guide her to Tom, not in the blackness of this night. The heat of panic burned in her throat and her eyes crinkled, threatening tears.

Then — a pale light, bobbing and dodging in the trees ahead of her. A will o' the wisp? Something else? Should she be frightened? How could she save Tom if she panicked? Or couldn't find the bridge? A warm breeze came up, carrying a delicate and familiar fragrance to her nostrils. The rose — Tom's rose — that was the scent. Dancer snorted.

"You smell it too, don't you, old friend," she whispered. "Shall we try to follow the light?" The will o' the wisp, a mother-of-pearl glow, drew near and dodged away, came close again and once more moved ahead. The second time, she followed.

At last they came to the bridge. The will o' the wisp blinked out. The lighted dial of Lily's wristwatch told her that it was still half an hour before midnight. She tethered Dancer some distance away. Taking the blanket she'd tied to her saddle, she hid herself as best she could in the brush close by the bridge. As if to mock her and her poor attempt at concealment, the bright moon emerged from the clouds. Every nerve on edge, she waited.

It seemed like she'd been there for hours when Dancer neighed and she heard another horse whinny in reply. Then she heard bells, multitudes of silvery bells singing together. She knew the sound meant many riders. And then she saw the Fair Folk for the first time.

At the head of the procession rode a tall, slender, pale woman on a grey horse. That had to be the Queen of Faerie. She wore a crown of flowers atop hair so palely golden it was like gilt and a long, form-fitting dress of leaf-green silk, its skirt divided for riding. A proud falcon balanced on her wrist. The Queen was so beautiful she made Lily's heart ache. If this woman wanted Tom, what chance did she, Lily, have against her?

Following the Queen rode a disorderly troop of men and women, all nearly as beautiful as their ruler, with hawks on their wrists and hunting dogs running alongside their horses. How was she to tell which one among them was Tom?

Think, Lily. Remember. She could almost hear his voice. "Because I was a mortal man of some accomplishment, she always makes me ride just behind her. You'll know me by my own white mare and by the rose I've fastened to the bridle."

As the riders neared she studied each one closely. There was Tom's mare, she was sure, and yes, there was the rose. No other rider had such a flower.

The troop approached the bridge, bells jingling, hooves tapping, silvery voices rising in ethereal song. Lily sprang out from her hiding place just as Tom's horse set foot on the bridge and grabbed her lover by the arm. Surprise gave her the advantage — he lost his balance and fell toward her. She pulled him free of his stirrups, and they fell to the ground tangled up in each other. Quickly she wrapped both her arms around him and held him as tightly as she could.

The procession halted. The Queen wheeled her horse around, staring into the night until she saw Lily and Tom.

"You shall not have him," the Queen shrieked, and in Lily's arms the man she held was transformed into a writhing, fanged snake as strong as she, striking wildly at her. Terrified, she almost let go. Her hands slid on the dry scales, and the snake nearly broke free. But somehow under the patterned snakeskin she could feel Tom's own body, his warm smooth skin, his own powerful muscles, and she held fast.

How long? She had no idea. But when she felt she could hold no more, there was another transformation. For one brief moment, she beheld Tom himself, clad in the finest clothes of Faerie. Then he was gone, and in his place was a mountain lion with claws capable of ripping her apart and teeth that could shatter bones. The lion roared at her, but in its wild gaze she could still recognize her lover's deep-seeing blue eyes. She clung to the fierce animal with an unrelenting grip.

It got worse. In succession the writhing lion she held became a creature with a lizard's head and a bear's body; then something that resembled a small dragon, threatening her with beating leathery wings and poisonous fire; then a unicorn seeking to impale her with a horn sharp as a sword. She prayed for strength and held on. Under the attacks of a creature that seemed half man, half lion her legs gave out and she fell. But she remembered that this was only Tom, the father of her child, and she managed to pin the thing under her own body until she got a new hold on it and could pull herself to her feet.

A heartbeat later all the writhing and struggling stopped. She found herself clutching a hard bar of iron, cold and dead. She could no longer sense Tom anywhere. At that moment she almost forgot everything he had told her, all his warnings and all his advice. She thought she had lost, and she nearly flung the dead thing away. Blinking away tears, she looked up—and caught a glimpse of the Queen. The beautiful woman of Faerie sat her horse proudly, with a look of both victory and contempt on her cold face. And Lily remembered that Taylor had looked at her with very nearly the same expression when the two accidentally met on the street, after Taylor had won Kevin away. She felt her own face harden. Tom was not Kevin. He was worth fighting for. She was going to win this time. She hung on.

Then somewhere in the distance, she heard a rooster crow. The Queen heard it too. As the rooster's call died away, she raised her hand and pointed a finger at Lily. The bar of iron coalesced into a lump of black coal, which then caught fire. And Lily knew her battle was won. As Tom had told her to do, she threw the coal into the stream beside the bridge. No sooner had the glow of fire spluttered out when Tom himself arose naked from the water, dripping and dazed. She seized the blanket she had brought, threw it over his shoulders, wrapped him in it as best she could and hugged him to her. The rooster crowed again.

The Queen shrieked, "You have stolen away from me the fairest of all my lovers. I curse you both with an evil death, you and your children after you." Her extended hand shook and her voice trembled with anger.

But Lily saw the pain in her eyes and the ghost of a tear on the immortal woman's pale cheek.

"Queen. Sister. Dear sister," she said. "Your curses can't harm me, for I call upon God to shield me and mine. Like me, who am your mortal kin, you have loved well but not wisely, and your love for Tom Linn was not meant to be. But you have loved, and for that God blesses you and I forgive you, for you are God's creatures too, you and those who ride with you."

The rooster crowed once more, lustily. All the anger suddenly fled the Queen's face and instead there came an expression of surprise and then calm. "Truly so many years have passed I thought God had abandoned us. But you have brought us a different message, and now I know better. I feel it. At last I feel once more the Father's touch upon me and upon my people. Go, little sister. You are braver than any mortal I have ever known, and you have earned the right to a peaceful life with your man and your child to be." She raised a graceful hand, signaling her retinue to follow, and then all the horses and their riders faded into transparency as the rising sun burned off the mists. But Lily heard the Queen say one more thing, a faint message carried on the morning breeze. "We do not forsake our own, and now both of you belong to us as well as to the mortals. We are leaving this realm for a time, but it is not forever. Watch for us at dusk on a night when the moon is full." Then the jubilant morning chorus of the songbirds overwhelmed the sound of whispering silver bells.

As harrowing as the night's experience had been for Lily, it had obviously been worse for Tom. He was wet and cold from the dousing in the creek, shivering even though he was wrapped in the blanket. He was smiling, though, laughing and shaking all at once. Fighting her weariness, Lily managed to help him up onto Dancer's back, and they rode wearily back to the farmhouse. Lily unsaddled Dancer and turned him out into the meadow. Much to her surprise, Tom's white mare Paloma was already there.

Inside, Lily kindled a fire in the big fieldstone fireplace, then heated up bowls of hot chicken soup on the stove for Tom and herself. Though the day promised to be a lovely one, both man and woman were too exhausted to care. Soon they crawled under the bedcovers together and slept the next twenty-four hours away.

Lily woke first, to sunlight and the warm scent of the roses outside the window. The first thing she did was reach over to touch Tom, making sure he was still there. "We're safe, we're together," she whispered to herself. "We're home."

"I heard that," he said, rolling over and kissing her. "We're forever now, Lily, you and I. Now come and enjoy the prize you've won."

"Egotist!" she said, laughing, and she did.

Epilogue

With Lily's victory and the passing of the Faerie troop, the farm once more lay open to the outside world. At first it wasn't easy for Tom. A great deal had changed since the Faerie Queen had taken him. Sprawling suburbs had sprung up where farms once flourished; a tangle of highways new to him now were congested with cars capable of going faster than any he remembered. Families he had once known were gone. The map of the world had changed dramatically, and so had political alliances. He had to relearn a great deal of what he had once known. But he was eager to become a vital part of the times in which he found himself.

Lily introduced him to the city and the people that she knew, and together they met their near neighbors, who forever remained puzzled about the sudden appearance of a farm that had seemingly not been there before.

Tom insisted on their marriage, and so they journeyed to Kentucky, where Lily's parents, her sisters and her brother witnessed the ceremony.

As heir to his parents' wealth, Tom did not lack for money, and he poured it into restoring their house and farm. The winter in that first enchanted year was mild and slowed their efforts only a little. In February their first child was born, a son. They named him Will in memory of Tom's father.

In the spring, Tom's mare foaled. The colt was silver white like her, with reddish ears and stockings. He became the foundation sire for a line of horses envied by every horseman for miles around.

Do lovers who found each other in a fairy tale live happily ever after?

Truth be told, any married couple will disagree. And so did Lily and Tom, now and then. Yet their life was a happy one. Tom concentrated on raising horses and cultivating the orchards of cherry and apple trees. Lily swore she was done with writing, but it was in her blood and soon she took up pen — or rather computer — and began composing magazine articles and short stories until finally her hard work was rewarded with publication. At length she managed one successful novel and then another.

More children were born, until there were two daughters and another son. The children grew up and attended good schools, married and went away, all except for Will. Maybe because he had been conceived while the land was still under the enchantment of Faerie, the boy had always loved the farm, the animals and the orchards. When he married he brought his bride home to the old farmstead.

By then Lily's well-loved old gelding Dancer had died, and one day Tom's mare Paloma vanished from her paddock and was never seen again. While they always had plenty of fine horses to ride, none ever claimed their hearts like the two that had been so much a part of their courtship and first love.

In the fullness of time there were grandchildren and then great-grandchildren. Lily and Tom had lived to a great age, and their bodies at long last grew weak and fragile. So on summer evenings, they sat together on cushions on a wicker couch in front of the old marble fountain, holding hands and watching the fireflies dance and the moon rise.

One evening they fell asleep together out there and did not wake until midnight, so pleasant and warm was the night. The scent of roses perfumed the air. A full moon had risen and was now high in the sky, among stars so brilliant the old couple thought they were still dreaming, because their fading eyesight could no longer perceive anything as tiny as a distant star.

In the old farmhouse, something woke Will, and he went to the open window of the bedroom he shared with his wife. He would have called out to his mother and father, but before he did he heard the silvery chiming of tiny bells. He stood still, watching.

Lily had heard it too. She squeezed Tom's bony old hand and he woke. A light mist rose from the grass. It parted to reveal the Queen of Faerie, mounted on her red-eared grey stallion. She held two white horses by their lead reins. Lily would have sworn that one of the two animals was her old bay, Dancer, and the other Tom's mare, Paloma.

"You gave me your blessing," the Queen said to Lily, "and you forgave me the evils I would have committed. And you reminded me of something that we, in our pride, had almost forgotten — that we too are God's creatures. So as I promised I have come back for you both. Here are your horses — ride with us."

Lily and Tom, their limbs unexpectedly supple and light, arose and mounted, taking up their reins. One of the queen's knights fastened soft mist-gray cloaks around their shoulders. Will, watching, saw his parents as they must have looked so many years ago when they were young.

"We will follow in the moon's path," said the Queen. The horses stepped off, the bells on the bridles sounded, and then all grew quiet except for the chirrup of the cricket at home under the rose bushes.

love is pleasin'
—sometimes

The female of the species
is more deadly than the male.

— Rudyard Kipling

Picture Me Wealthy

The friggin' establishment, the authorities who made sure you did what they wanted you to do–made me, Brandy Hampton, what I am today. That's not my real name–my birth certificate reads "Carleen Rose Fischer"–but I erased that name a nanosecond after I lit out from Fort Wayne, Indiana, where I grew up.

Go to elementary school and sit still, the establishment demanded. Don't chew gum, don't get caught passing notes, don't draw dirty pictures in your notebook when your teacher is carrying on about verb forms or the battles of the Civil War. Go to Sunday school and make sure you keep your dress clean. Go to high school, make yourself popular, stay out of trouble, don't get pregnant, become a cheerleader–well, not that last thing, it was me who wanted to become a cheerleader, but of course the authorities allowed for a little bit of fun within that ugly red brick building they called a high school. High school? You couldn't buy drugs for miles around. The establishment made sure of it. I could always get 'em, though, 'cause my Ma knew the right people. That sure helped with my popularity.

I did what the authorities wanted me to do. I went to high school, and I took the business classes because Ma thought I could make a living as an administrative assistant and support her when her looks failed her totally. She drank so much and did so many drugs that it wouldn't be long before her looks were gone.

Administrative assistant–that's the fancy new name for what they used to call a secretary, like the building engineer used to be called the custodian used to be called the janitor. The establishment thinks they can bamboozle us with fancy job titles, but the truth is that these are still low-pay, low-prestige, no-power jobs for nobodies like me. Ma insisted that I couldn't follow her into her profession because I wasn't pretty like she was once. The mirror told me different and so did the leering glances of the pot-bellied, bald-headed men who visited Ma just about every night, but I didn't want to earn my way entertaining them. What else could I do? I guess that's why I was training for dead-end jobs like administrative assistant.

Some nights Ma and her gentlemen friends woke me up with their yelling and moaning. When that happened, I knew I'd get no sleep, so I watched the action through the little peephole I'd drilled through my bedroom wall with a nail file–tangles of arms and legs, breasts and balls, squirming, clawing and hitting and biting and laughing and crying. I knew what it was about, all right. I was mature for my age–who wouldn't be, with a hooker for a mother? The next day I'd take out my pencils and draw pictures of what I'd seen. Got pretty good at it too, and I had lots of different male models. But Ma always looked the same except she got skinnier and bonier and sicklier.

I graduated from high school somewhere in the middle of my class, but I still didn't want to be an administrative assistant. So while Ma thought I was looking for a job, I was hanging out at the big mall over across town and doing what I call studying human behavior. I watched shoppers in action. It's amazing how many people let their purses hang open or their wallets sit out on the counters. I had clever hands, and before long I discovered that I could snatch rich folks' cash from right under their noses. It was so easy I could picture myself getting wealthy, and for awhile it seemed I was right. Within a few months I'd managed to steal a few thousand dollars–man, I felt rich–but then one night a nosy old lady caught me with my fingers in her handbag.

Well, she let out a screech to wake the dead and grabbed my wrist. I yelped and yanked my hand away so hard she fell down. I ran, dodging startled shoppers, bolting out of the nearest entrance and hiding among the cars in the parking lot until the security goons gave up looking for me. They didn't try very hard. Nobody got hurt and I didn't get the old bat's money, so I guess they didn't care if I got away.

I figured that was the end of my shopping expeditions to the mall. I needed a bigger place in which I could exercise my special talents. So I snuck back home, where Ma was entertaining her nightly boyfriend. The two of them were rockin' and rollin' in the bedroom and didn't hear a thing when I tossed my sketchbooks and a few clothes into a shopping bag and cleaned out Ma's ill-earned wealth from its hiding place in the back of the broom closet, adding it to my own considerable stash.

The john had dropped his pants on the floor in what passed for our living room, and – hot damn! – there was a wallet and a set of car keys in them. Taking both, I slipped out the back door and climbed into the car parked outside our place. It was an old Monte Carlo with dirty plastic duct-taped over the hole where the passenger side window used to be, but its engine started right up when I turned the key in the ignition. Just like that, I was on my way to bigger things.

I drove and drove that night. I figured the cops might be looking for me and the car I'd stolen, so as soon as I could I ditched the Monte Carlo in the parking lot at an all-night bar and found myself another set of wheels with the keys forgotten in the ignition.

A couple more stolen cars and some hitchhiking got me to New York City. It was so big and crowded that I thought could pick pockets for the rest of my life and never get caught. But after I'd been filching wallets for a year or so, a street-smart cop caught me with my hand in an unsuspecting gent's back pocket. Since it was a first offense, I got off easy, but I knew it was time to quit the street life. By then I had more important things to do anyway. I had discovered a better way to get rich, and it was perfectly legal.

You see, all those nights that I'd watched Ma and her johns go at it and then made sketches of their more inventive antics paid off. Since I'd landed in New York, I'd used some of my ill-gotten gains to pay for some art courses. In art school, I learned that what I thought were just dirty pictures were actually fine examples of what my drawing instructor called "erotica" and could be very valuable–to the right people. I expanded my technique to painting, and soon my fellow students, my instructors and their friends were beating a path to my easel. Before long, I had my own gallery. A long list of patrons who desired works painted by the notorious Brandy Hampton were making me wealthy.

Now, when I've put the last brushstrokes on a painting that will sell for a tidy sum, I crook a finger at my very own administrative assistant. I chose one who's handsome and obliging. He knows what that crooked finger means, and he rushes to fetch glasses of champagne for us both. I laugh as we toast the idiots who made me what I am today–doctors, lawyers, politicians, corporate executives–even school principals, and every one a platinum credit card-carrying member of the establishment.

Cheers!

The Mule Kicker

W ith ten minutes left before class, the cool guys in their blue and gold letter jackets clustered in the main hall of Willard High. Playfully punching each other's shoulders, they whistled at the girls passing by and received smiles in return.

At the edge of the raucous gathering, Larry Kline attempted a joke. Nobody paid any attention. He grimaced. He wasn't welcome in the inner circle. He wanted to be one of the big men on campus. But he didn't play football, and his intellect was merely average. More damning, he lived with his mother in a trailer park by the railroad yard. He didn't fit in.

Larry had one thing going for him. He had his own car, and the other guys sometimes asked him for a ride when they wanted to go someplace special. He guessed that was why they tolerated him. He'd worked long hours as a stock boy at Food Town, and by the time he turned 16, he'd saved enough cash to buy a rusty old Ford sedan. It ran okay, and he didn't have to depend on a father's good will when he wanted to drive. 'Course his dad was long gone, killed in Vietnam a year after Larry was born.

The guys were talking about which girls would put out and which ones were ice princesses. Would they be impressed enough to accept him if he could get to first base with one of the icy ones? It would have to be a popular girl. But what popular girl would give him the time of day?

The clangor of the hall bell ended Larry's musings. He hustled to his geometry class. He liked math and usually concentrated when the teacher explained the lesson, but today he found himself distracted by a girl he'd never noticed before.

A sweet-faced pixie, that's what she reminded him of, an elf with shiny brown hair and blue eyes. She wore a blue and white striped blouse that Larry recognized as a "distinction," a garment selected by each high school sorority to identify their members. The blouse marked her as one of the in-crowd. In class, she was quiet–a little frightened of the math. Maybe he could help her–that would be a first step toward asking her out.

After school, he caught up with her at the bus stop. "Hey, what's your name?" he asked.

"Oh, I know you," she said. "You're in my geometry class. My name's Margaret Baldwin, but everybody calls me Maggie."

"Having a little trouble with math?" Larry inquired.

"It's hard for me," she admitted. "I don't understand what Mr. Hauser was talking about today."

"Well, if you don't have to get home right away, I could go over the lesson with you."

"That'd be nice," she said, "but I have to take this bus home. It'll be a long time before another one comes, and it's too far for me to walk."

"No problem. I can drive you. Suppose we go over to the Dairy Bar and talk about it over a malted."

Maggie surprised him by saying yes. She must really be desperate to get a good grade in geometry, he thought.

After a week of after-hours math lessons, Larry risked asking Maggie out. She agreed to a movie date, and that Saturday night, he picked her up at her house. But instead of going to the theater, he drove out along the river road.

"Where are we going?" she asked.

"A nice place I know. You'll see."

"Okay, I guess. As long as I get home by midnight."

A few miles down the road, Larry steered into a dark lane. The car bounced along the ruts until they reached a flat spot where they could see out over the river.

"Pretty here, ain't it," he said as he turned the engine off. "How about a kiss?" Maggie didn't resist when he pulled her closer and touched her half-opened lips with his tongue.

I'm on my way, he thought, and placed his hand on her breast, stroking it through the soft wool of her sweater. She jumped as though startled but allowed him to reach under her sweater and her bra to the soft flesh underneath. Bingo!

"Get in the back seat," he whispered.

She sat up abruptly, pulling his hand away from her breast. "No," she said. "I won't do that."

"Don't be a tease. Get in the back seat or get out and walk."

Maggie stared at him. Larry stared back. His groin was throbbing with urgency.

She opened the car door and jumped out, pulling her sweater down. Turning her back on him, she marched off down the dark road. He had to run to catch her.

"You get back here," Larry growled, grabbing her shoulder with one hand. She spun to face him, dislodging his hand, and planted a powerful kick in his crotch. He doubled over, clutching his balls and gasping for breath. When he could talk again, he yelled, "Now you're gonna get it. Just wait… "

But Maggie had vanished into the darkness.

He climbed painfully back into the car, massaging his groin. He'd catch her – damn, where were the car keys? Not in the ignition, not in his pocket, not on the car seat, not on the floor. He got out again and crawled in the weeds until his searching hands located the errant keys.

Once he got the jalopy started, Larry raced back to the main road. No sign of the little slut. Well, he'd have his revenge. Wait until he told the guys the story – his way. He'd ruin her reputation for good.

First thing on Monday morning, he swaggered up to the cluster of popular guys. "Hey, listen to this–that Maggie Baldwin, that holier-than-thou sorority bitch – I had her Saturday night. And she was great, let me tell you, all hot for me. You wouldn't believe…"

"You bet we wouldn't believe," said Jim Eakins, the first-string quarterback. "Pete, tell him what your dad said."

Pete Novak, a tackle on the football team, let a big slow grin spread across his ugly mug. "You can't fool us, Kline. My Dad met up with Maggie at the Sunoco station out on the river road Saturday night. She told him she was running away from you, and she told him exactly why. He took her home. By the way, how do your balls feel today?"

Several of the other guys chuckled.

"Don't you know we call Maggie 'Magpie the Mule Kicker?'" asked Jim. "Nobody's had her yet, and nobody's going to. She's a real mule kicker, that one. You're not the first jerk she's booted. If we could only get her on the football team, we could win the league championship."

Maybe it was the look on his face that set them all to laughing. Or maybe the red flush he could feel rising up from his neck. Whatever it was, when the bell for classes sounded, the guys turned away from him, guffawing. As they sauntered down the hall, he heard someone shout "Yaaay, Magpie!" and snicker.

Feeling like a leper, Larry stood alone. He saw Maggie and a couple of her girlfriends approaching. A smile, a dismissive wave of her hand, and she went on her way. To geometry class. If he waited any longer, the hallway monitor would be on him. He slunk after the girls, "Mule Kicker! Magpie! Mule Kicker!" relentlessly resounding in his head.

it's a hard life

Sometimes I feel like a motherless child
A long way from home.

— Traditional folk song

Esperanza's Sorrow

On the April day when two uniformed patrolmen knocked on the front door of her Rogers Park bungalow, Esperanza Marchita Marquez knew that they had come to confirm the fear that had haunted her for the past three months – the fear that her only child was lost to her forever.

The taller of the two introduced himself. "Mrs. Marquez, I'm Sergeant Hector Diaz, a homicide detective for Chicago police department, and this is my partner, Jesse Reyes. I'm so sorry..."

Esperanza clasped her hands together and raised them to her mouth, praying that she might awake and find that her nightmare had fled in the light of a new day.

"I'm so very sorry," Sergeant Diaz continued. "On a tip from one of our informants, we located the remains of a young man and a young woman in a Glenview retention pond. Our crime investigation unit has identified the woman as your daughter, Narcisa. The male was a known drug dealer. We believe both were murdered, though we don't have an autopsy report as yet."

Esperanza did not shriek at the news, nor did she weep, although she felt her heartbeat stutter, and for a long moment she could not speak. But then her renegade heart resumed its steady rhythm, insisting that her life continue despite the death of her beloved 18-year-old daughter. Willing her emotions to be still, Esperanza quietly thanked the officers for their concern.

When the officers had driven away, Esperanza did what she always did in times of trouble: She went into her little dressmaking studio, where she had spent years sewing fine apparel for some of the city's wealthiest women. Inside, lengths of fabric were stacked neatly upon shelves; garments in progress hung on racks; and sewing machines and sergers waited on tables, ready to be called upon.

Esperanza didn't know what she intended to do in the studio until her hand fell upon her keenest pair of shears. Taking them up, she went next to Narcisa's room, where she pulled her daughter's garments from the closet and spread them out on the bed. All the colors of a summer garden, all the colors of youth, she thought. So beautiful, as her wayward Narcisa had been.

Tears would not come. Esperanza raised her shears and began cutting Narcisa's skirts into random pieces. The newer skirts were so short and the tops so skimpy that there was scarcely enough fabric in them to make her efforts worthwhile. All the girls wore clothes like these, Narcisa had assured her. It was the American way. Esperanza had believed her daughter. What did a mother so far from her birthplace in Michoacan know about what was right for girls in this cold and alien city?

She picked up Narcisa's prom dress. Narcisa had made it herself, a sophisticated gown in shades of turquoise and ecru. Esperanza glanced at her daughter's dresser, where Narcisa beamed from a photo in which she was wearing the dress and standing beside her prom date, Jorge Ramirez. Jorge was a nice young man, not like the *Norteamericano* punks Narcisa had been seeing lately. Esperanza's shears slashed into the dress, severing threads of memories. Next came the ivory-white dress from Narcisa's *quinceanara*, the festive celebration of her fifteenth birthday. Esperanza sighed as her scissors reduced it to scraps. The sharp blades made short work of Narcisa's gray and navy blue school uniforms, of her pastel Sunday dresses and of her flowered nightgowns.

By the time Esperanza finished cutting, the streetlights were casting their harsh orange light into the darkened neighborhood. Esperanza piled the scraps of Narcisa's short life into brown paper bags, lay down upon her daughter's bed and slept.

Daylight awakened Esperanza. She rose from Narcisa's bed and went to the bathroom to splash water on her face and then to the kitchen. There she fried up a plate of *huevos* and tortillas, forcing herself to eat before taking the bags of newly cut scraps to her dressmaking studio. The task she had set herself would require strength.

Esperanza owned several newer sewing machines, each one more electronically elaborate than the next, but she chose to sit down instead at her old Kenmore. She had bought that machine soon after she and her husband, Carlos, got married, five years before Narcisa's birth. Carlos had made good money working construction jobs until the night he went out with his friends and drank a little too much. After he left the bar, he crashed his pickup truck into a viaduct. His darling Narcisa had just reached her second birthday.

With Carlos gone, Esperanza used her sewing skills to become a custom dressmaker. She worked hard with that Kenmore machine and managed to provide herself and Narcisa with an adequate living. Now she selected a cone of daffodil-yellow thread and inserted it into the machine's needle. The machine was ready.

Esperanza fingered the scraps of fabric in one of the brown paper bags, lifting out a random dozen. She took a blue polka-dotted cotton patch–a piece of Narcisa's favorite Sunday dress–and stitched it to a multicolored swatch of tropical print cut from a swimsuit cover-up. She added a semicircle of lime-green linen that had recently been part of a skirt. Then she sewed on a bright red scrap, fabric from one of Narcisa's first sewing projects. As she guided the pieces under the needle, grief flowed from Esperanza's heart down her arms and through her fingers into the thread and the fabrics and the bed of the sewing machine. The machine throbbed imperceptibly as each unshed tear reached it, and microscopic flakes of its plastic casing broke loose and fell to the table.

The doorbell rang around ten in the morning, interrupting Esperanza's desperate patchwork. It was Father McCarthy, the parish priest, calling to offer his condolences and to discuss a funeral mass for Narcisa. At the priest's urging, Esperanza telephoned the director of the funeral home she'd chosen. He found time in the day's schedule to help her select a casket and plan the visitation. She left with a sample of the golden satin that would cushion Narcisa's eternal bed.

By the time Esperanza returned to her house, the daylight was almost gone. She reheated a bowl of leftover *picadillo* and ate it sitting in front of her television set, watching stolidly as the news channel broadcast videos of the scene where Narcisa's body had been found. Again that night she slept in her daughter's room as though she could absorb her child's essence from the bed in which the girl had slept.

Early the next morning, Esperanza resumed her patient stitching. The satin sample from yesterday's visit to the funeral home was the first piece she added to her slowly growing patchwork. Her sorrow flowed with the fabric into the machine, but unlike the stitched pieces, it never emerged from under the presser foot. It chipped away at the Kenmore's bobbin mechanisms, its tension controls, its feed dogs, its wiring and its gears.

After Narcisa's burial, Esperanza's days took on a routine. She rose early in the morning and worked for a while on the patchwork of scraps. Now and then a tear she'd been unable to suppress dropped onto the Kenmore and vanished into its workings. When that happened, the rise and fall of the needle hesitated imperceptibly, then resumed its rhythmic motion.

Around ten most mornings, one client or another would call with a request. Despite her sorrow, Esperanza could not afford to say no. Most difficult were the days when mothers brought their lovely young daughters to be fitted for their coming-out dresses. Now and then Esperanza would select scraps of fabric left over from the construction of these festive gowns and stitch them into her patchwork.

Sometimes the police detective, Sergeant Diaz, called to bring Esperanza up to date on the investigation into Narcisa's murder. The police were working on it but had nothing definite as yet. But they would solve the case, of that he was certain. Sergeant Diaz was a Chicano, and Esperanza trusted him because he spoke to her in Spanish.

Every evening after her supper, Esperanza walked to the cemetery. If the florist on Ridge Avenue was open, she bought flowers. At first it was narcissus, Narcisa's namesake flower. As spring moved into summer, it would be daisies or glads. Sometimes she laid a single yellow rose on Narcisa's grave. Then she knelt on the grass and prayed for justice.

As autumn approached, Esperanza's patchwork fabric took on a vaguely rectangular shape. Piecing it together was slow work because she had cut the scraps so small, but she felt no urgency. Esperanza didn't notice that her reliable Kenmore sewing machine had developed rust spots here and there, nor that its once-glossy case had become discolored and shabby as her fingers continued to release more and more of her grief into her work. She saw only her careful lines of stitching and the bits of Narcisa's garments she used. There were swatches from the ivory *quinceanara* dress interspersed with strips from a flowered pink blouse, navy oblongs from a school uniform, a scrap of blue bathrobe, and fragments of a very old T-shirt printed all over with images of Snoopy. The sewing machine soldiered on, putting thousands of stitches into the patchwork history of Narcisa's brief life.

When all the scraps had been sewn together, Esperanza cut a piece of polyester batting to fit the patchwork rectangle. For backing, she took a piece of Narcisa's yellow bedspread. She basted the layers of patchwork, batting and backing together on the Kenmore. Then she began stitching the lines of quilting. It seemed random at first, but before long the lines resolved into interlaced outlines of narcissus blossoms. Every stitch diminished her grief by a fraction, although Esperanza did not yet recognize that.

Late in the afternoon on a chilly November day, Sergeant Diaz came to Esperanza's bungalow. He told her that Narcisa's killers had been caught–four young men who trafficked in all manner of illegal substances.

"*Norteamericano*?" Esperanza timidly asked.

"No, Colombian gangbangers," Diaz said. "They shot your daughter and her boyfriend and threw their bodies into that Glenview pond."

"These young people, no good," muttered Esperanza. "Doesn't matter where they come from. Will they go to jail? What will happen to them?"

"They'll be in jail for a while, and then they'll go to trial," Sergeant Diaz told her. "Maybe they'll be convicted. Maybe not. Sometimes, if they can pay for a good lawyer, they get off. These Colombians, now, they have money—"

"Where is justice?" Esperanza asked.

Diaz shook his head. "It's in God's hands," he said.

On the following day, Esperanza sewed the final stitches into the quilt she had assembled from memories of her daughter's life. When she had finished, she released the quilt from the old Kenmore machine. It was hard to raise the presser foot, and the corroded mechanism dropped dull metallic shards on the fabric when it finally relaxed its grip. She lifted the cloth from the machine and tied off the last line of stitching.

The finished piece was an artistic masterpiece, but to Esperanza, its beauty resided only in what it represented—what she had been able to salvage of her daughter's severed life. Standing up, she shook out the fabric and wrapped it around herself. As its warmth enveloped her, her tears finally flowed.

But as Esperanza made peace with her sorrow and regained hope, the old Kenmore sewing machine broke down. The presser foot fell off its corroded mounting, dropping to the rusted needle plate with a nearly inaudible click. The tension discs froze in place, immobilizing the thread path. A massive Gordian knot jammed the workings of the bobbin case. The hand wheel stalled, and the teeth of the gears sheared off. A network of fine cracks spread through the shabby plastic case. The filament in the machine's lightbulb crumbled, and the light went out.

The old Kenmore had struggled to take away Esperanza's grief. When its work was completed and it could do no more, it perished of sorrow – Esperanza's sorrow.

Some Kinda Miracle

Not much left here to stay for, just this shack I built out of cheap two by fours and walled in with scraps of wood, cardboard and sheets of newspaper. That's all we have for a house. Not a tree for a hundred miles around, or I'd'a built us a better home. We had a sod house once, but the dust blew in and just about filled it up. No point in going back to it.

The well still works. It's deep. I haul buckets from the pump out back, keep it in a drum outside, near the kitchen. It was supposed to be a rain barrel, but it never got no rain in it. Takes a lot of trips to the well just to get enough water to wash dishes and the few clothes we have. Once a week or so I haul enough to give us all a bath–Emma, little Dottie, and me. Don't take much water to give Joey a bath–he's just a few months old. Emma's been frail since Joey was born. She's all worn out from washing and cooking and having babies–she lost two between Dottie and Joey.

Hasn't rained in three years. Every year I plowed and planted wheat. Every year it died of heat and drought. Jack rabbits come down out of the mountains this year and ate every little green shoot they could find. All us men and boys got together and drove hundreds of 'em into pens. Clubbed 'em to death. Emma says she can still hear 'em crying as they died. Dottie just runs out of the house when she hears her Ma talk that way, goes out behind the shack and bawls. I let her cry for awhile, then I go pick her up and bring her back into the shack. She's almost eight years old, but I can still carry her. Skin and bones. I try to soothe her down.

I was one of the lucky ones. I sold my stock–my team of horses and the two milk cows–while they was still sound. Got enough cash to buy us a car. I hear the government men are coming now to shoot the rest of the cattle in this part of Colorado. Maybe it's better than lettin' 'em starve to death. You know what, though? I can still see our gentle Bessie, her kind eye, and how good she was, givin' us her milk. I think the folk who bought our cows was gonna slaughter 'em for dog food. I didn't say nothin' about it.

Emma keeps asking, What'd we do so bad that God is punishing us like this? All we did was plow and plant. We got such good crops at first, too. Now them black storms roll in. No rain, all black dust. In

our eyes, our noses, our mouths. That last storm–
Emma thought the world was coming to an end.

I didn't tell her I thought so too.

Some folks think this can't last, that it's going to
get better. Over t' the next county, they hired 'em a
man who said he could make it rain by explodin' dy-
namite in the ground, sendin' up more dust with
every explosion. Well, maybe it worked. We got a
little snow after he done three tries. But that was a
year ago, and ain't been no snow or rain since.

Had some money put by from the good years,
but it's just about gone. Bank gave us all some cash
to buy some groceries–federal relief, said Lyle Trav-
ers–he's the bank president. Thanks, I said, but it
won't last long. I'm leaving, going back east where
I've got some family and the crops still grow.

Not California? Lyle asked me. Most folks are
headed west. Charley, they all say California's the
promised land, a land of real milk and honey.

Well, yeah, that's what they told me about this
patch of desert I'm tryin' to farm. For a couple of
years, it was. Then everything dried up. That don't
happen back in Pennsylvania, least not much. 'Sides,
I still got family there. My brother Walt sent me a
telegram. Come on home, he says. I can use an extra
hand, he says.

Think about it, says Lyle. You decide to go, I'll
give you a full tank of gas, just like I done for everyone else who left.

I thought about it too long. Emma started to
cough and then she got a fever. She took to her bed–
wasn't no help for it. Little Dottie tried to help,
watchin' over Joey, changing his diapers, stirring up
pots of watery bean soup with what little food we

had. I sat with Emma day and night, puttin' wet cloths on her forehead–she was burnin' hot. Pretty soon she was coughin' up thick phlegm and blood too. It was the dust pneumonia for sure.

A week after she started coughin', my Emma, my blue-eyed darling, left me. She slipped away from this world as I held her in my arms. First time since I was a little boy, I cried. And I cried. It was Dottie who tried to console me. She knew her Ma was gone–she's in the arms of Jesus now, Dottie said. Guess she learned that in Sunday school. It made her feel better. But I'd been praying to God for so many years now and got nothing for my praise and pleas but dirt. I have a hard time believin' anymore. Somewhere in the Bible it says that if you ask God the Father for bread, he won't give you a stone. Well, he didn't give us bread or a stone neither–just dust, dust like rainclouds rollin' in across the dry prairies–dust in our eyes, our noses, our mouths and our lungs.

I washed Emma's body and dressed her in her best calico gown. Her hair was clean and shiny for the first time in months. My neighbor, Frank Trimble, he had some planks, and he helped me build a coffin for Emma. Helped me dig the grave too. Preacher said a few words over her. Now Emma's resting at last, deep in this dry ground.

When it come right down to it, I couldn't just leave Emma behind, and I couldn't take her body back to Pennsylvania. So I stayed. Frank's wife, Fanny, helped me and Dottie take care of Joey until we could manage it on our own. We struggled for one more year.

Then one hot afternoon in May, the black clouds rose up on the western horizon. But this time it wasn't dust. Lightning flashed from the clouds to the ground. I could smell the rain on the wind as the clouds got closer. When the storm broke at last, I swear enough rain fell to fill up every dry creek and wash in all of Colorado and Oklahoma too. Dottie and I ran out of the shack and stood in the rain until it washed us and the ragged clothes we wore all clean. We laughed and danced in the falling water like fools. The roof leaked. I've never been happier to see water drippin' into pots on the floor and even on the beds.

We plowed. Lots of us didn't have horses any more, but them as had tractors came around and plowed for them as didn't. The government men had taught us how to plow so's to keep the soil from blowing away. We planted the wheat. The rains kept on a-comin,' and the little green shoots popped out of the earth and they grew. By fall the fields were all golden, ready to be harvested.

Some say it was a miracle. But I ask you, what kind of a miracle is it that took so many years of pain and grief before it happened?

With the rain, the ground over Emma's grave settled. I shoveled more dirt to fill in the hole, and then I went out onto a patch of fallow prairie and dug up the prettiest flowers I could find. I planted them on the grave.

Joey don't remember his ma. He was too young when she died. But Dottie and I tell him all about her. Just about every night, all three of us go out and sit on the green earth beside Emma. We talk to her, tell her how we're doin,' how much we miss her. A meadowlark flew out from the fields on one of those evenings, and her feathers brushed my cheek like an angel's wing.

I guess we're here to stay.

Sparrow on Whole Wheat

My name is Fern Girard, and I've lived in this apartment building for so many years that I've seen my Chicago neighborhood go from nice to rundown and back to up-and-coming. I've been here longer than anyone else in the building. I think that earns me some special consideration, don't you?

Today when I went out to the front hallway to get my mail, my next-door neighbor's copy of the Chicago *Tribune* was still lying in front of her door. It was almost noon, and if she'd wanted her paper, she'd have picked it up hours ago. So I swiped it.

I sat down at my kitchen table and opened the paper to the comics section, taking an occasional sip of vodka from the bottle so I wouldn't have to wash a glass. I was feeling nice and mellow. But then I decided to crack open the kitchen window, the one that looks out onto the courtyard, to get some fresh air.

Wouldn't you know, the first thing I saw was Shadrach, the evil black tomcat that belongs to my neighbors, the Morleys. He'd caught a sparrow, and I watched him toss the bird into the air with one clever paw. The bird flapped down to the winter-killed grass, ran a few steps and tried to lift off. Before it could escape, Shadrach swatted it down with his other paw and began chewing on a mangled wing.

That was the last straw. I'd put up with the cat's bird-killing far too long. It made me furious. I heaved myself out of my chair, bumping the table and knocking over my vodka bottle in the process. Most of the remaining contents spilled onto the kitchen floor. It was cheap booze, but it was all I had left, and that made me even angrier.

So I grabbed my broom and limped out of my kitchen door as fast as I could. Maybe I could still rescue the terrified sparrow from the cat-without-a-conscience.

Shadrach was crouched over his dying prey, looking up as if he dared me to do anything about it. I swung my broom at him. I wanted to kill him, I really did, so I brought the broom down with all the strength my old shoulders could muster, but Shadrach scooted out unharmed, the sparrow clenched in his teeth. The broom hit the frozen ground so hard it sent a jolt of pain right up through my wrists, all the way up my arms and into my head. I almost passed out.

Shadrach knew he'd won. He waltzed up to me, dropped the bleeding sparrow at my feet and ran off. I swear that cat was laughing at me.

I hated Shadrach, but right at that moment I hated his owners even more. Holier-than-thou S. Maxwell Morley and his long, skinny wife, Marcella Osborne Morley, let their several cats run free, even though I've complained time and time again that cats are filthy bird-murderers and should always be imprisoned indoors. But no. That bleeding liberal Max–as Mr. Morley prefers to be known–insists that cats have the God-given right to prowl. The God-given rights of birds don't cut any ice with him.

It's not like that black-hearted Shadrach kills because he's hungry. The only kind of bird he ever eats is processed chicken from a can.

Now all my vodka's gone, and I don't have the money to buy more. It's the Morleys' fault. They're as much to blame as their cat Shadrach.

Then I got a really bright idea that would stop Mister Max Morley and his foul feline in their self-righteous tracks. I picked up the dead sparrow by one foot and carried it into my apartment, where I set it on the kitchen counter. I had some nice china plates I'd found at a yard sale, and I picked one that had a rim lined with pretty little violets.

I hadn't bought food in a while. The Social Security check was later than usual this month. But I still had a loaf of whole wheat bread in the fridge. I took out a couple of slices and put one on the plate. I spooned mayonnaise on it until it oozed over the side of the bread, and I cut some lettuce leaves to fit precisely on top. Then I picked up the deceased sparrow and opened out its torn little wings so I could position it in the center of the lettuce. Its body was still warm, and a drop of its blood landed on the plate. I thought it made an appetizing splash of color. I topped it all with a second slice of bread and sliced a carrot into curls for garnish. Never let it be said that I didn't know how to make a good sandwich.

All that work was making me thirsty. I wanted some vodka. I picked up the fallen bottle and discovered that only a swallow remained. The rest had spilled onto the floor. Maybe it's a good thing my arthritis hurts so much that I can't get down on my knees. I needed a drink so bad I might have lapped it up off the linoleum. But I knew if I got down there I couldn't stand up again. I found a pencil and printed a note on the back of an unpaid electric bill. The note said, "Dear Max and Marcella, since your cat Shadrach caught this bird, he must have meant it for your lunch. So here is your bird sandwich. *Bon appetit.*" See, I'd been to college for a year, oh, a long time ago, and I knew a little French. Then I signed it, "Your friend, Fern Girard." Only I think I forgot the "r" in "friend."

Anyway, I took the plate over to the Morleys' back door – it's just a few steps away from mine in the apartment building – and set the plate down at their doorstep. Then I rang their doorbell and scooted back into my place to await the outcome of my little plan.

It wasn't long in coming. I heard a door open, and then a little shriek. That had to be the proper Marcella – a good loud scream wouldn't suit her. Just a little shriek. Then her composure deserted her, and she couldn't keep herself from yelling, "Max!

Max!" I peered out of my window and saw him come running. Who'd have thought an 80-year old drunk could move so fast?

I heard Max ask, "What's all this about?" Marcella turned to him and showed him the plate. He poked at the bird with his index finger. "It's still warm," he said in disgust.

"Fern did this!" Marcella held up my note and waved it under Max's red nose. "How could she? Aren't we her friends?"

I laughed out loud. I hope she heard me.

Then Marcella complained, at the top of her lungs, I might add, "Don't we get her groceries for her? Don't we buy her vodka? Isn't that enough? Why this – abomination? What does she want?"

Just as Marcella spoke, that black devil Shadrach streaked across the courtyard. I grabbed for my broom again, but the tomcat darted between Marcella's scrawny legs and ran into the Morleys' apartment. Good thing he did. I'd have been after him if he'd given me half a chance.

Alerted by the shouting, the nearest neighbors came out to see what was going on. That's one of the entertaining things about living in a cooperative apartment building. Everyone knows everyone else's business. There are no secrets. That busybody Ruth Jo Kramer who lives upstairs from me leaned out of her kitchen window. "Stop all this yelling! You woke me up from a nice nap!"

Well, I didn't feel sorry for her, not at all, that nosy old witch. I giggled.

Benjamin and Josh, the two queens who live next to Ruth Jo, pranced out onto their balcony and looked down at the scene. "What is that?" asked

Josh, pointing to the plate in Marcella's hand. "Why, I do believe it's a bird sandwich," observed Benjamin.

By now I was giggling uncontrollably. Guess the vodka was still working.

"Who'd make a sandwich for a bird?" asked Eduardo, whose apartment fronted on the opposite side of the courtyard."

"Not a sandwich for a bird," Josh corrected Eduardo. "A sandwich with bird filling. A sparrow sandwich, in fact." Eduardo didn't know what to say to that. He just stood there with his mouth open. A bird could have flown right into it.

Marcella was still standing frozen in her doorway, my lovely plate in her hand. Max patted her shoulder. "Well, my dear, what shall we do with this item?" he asked her.

"Just wait until I get my hands on that Fern!" Marcella raised her arm as if to throw the plate down and smash it, but Max stopped her before major damage was done. Then she sat down on the threshold, put the plate on her knees and burst into tears. "This is all so cruel," she sobbed. "I need a drink."

Well, so do I, lady, I thought. If your blasted cat hadn't killed that bird and made me knock over my bottle, I'd have one too. That *was* a crying matter. So I did just that–I sat back down at my kitchen table, put my face in my hands and bawled. My bird sandwich wouldn't bring back the bird. It wouldn't change Shadrach. Max and Marcella would have the last laugh. Now who would get my vodka for me?

I must have fallen asleep, because when I heard the doorbell ring, the kitchen was dark and only the electronic clock on the stove shed any light on the scene. The clock read 7:10. Morning or night? No idea. This time of year, it's dark at seven. Either seven.

I got up, slow, no other way I can get up considering how much my back aches and my knees hurt. It really gets to me. I used to be a dancer, good enough to get me a regular job in the chorus line at the old Chicago Theatre. Sometimes I dream I'm dancing, kicking just as high as I always did. When I wake up from that dream, I go straight for the bottle. I don't like remembering how it used to be.

The doorbell rang again. "C'mon, Fern, I know you're in there sulking."

It was S. Maxwell Morley.

"Go away, you bird murderer," I grumbled.

"Marcella made some chili and a batch of coconut cookies," he coaxed. "How about coming over for a bite to eat?"

I was hungry, but it wasn't just the food that sucked me in. The Morleys have vodka. They *always* have vodka. The two of them were the biggest lushes in the building. I knew I could get a drink there.

"Just a minute, please, I'm coming," I yelled. I opened the door and there stood Max, just as unrepentant as you please.

"Food's getting cold," said Max.

A few flakes of snow were falling. I took my coat from the hook by the door and wrapped it around my shoulders. At my age, one can't be too careful. If I catch a cold, it lasts for weeks.

Marcella greeted us at the kitchen door, just as sickeningly sweet as she could be. "Hi, Fern, glad to see you," she simpered, as if the gift of a dead-sparrow-on-whole-wheat sandwich was a fine thing, exactly what she might expect from a friend. "Come on in and get warm. Maybe you'd like a bowl of chili? And a drink before dinner?"

I hadn't eaten all day, and the chili smelled good, even if I had to kowtow to bird killers to get some of it. I sat down across the table from Marcella and Max, and Max put some ice cubes in a glass and poured in a whole lot of vodka. I grabbed it with both hands because my hands were shaking and took a big gulp.

Shadrach swaggered past me, tail high in the air, and stood expectantly at the kitchen door. Max reached over and pulled it open, and the black cat walked out, turning back to look at me with a smirk on his whiskered face.

When we'd polished off our chili, Marcella poured us all some more vodka and brought out the coconut cookies. They were neatly stacked on my flowered plate, the same one I'd put the sparrow sandwich on.

"Don't worry," Marcella said. "Max buried the bird in the courtyard, and I washed the plate in very hot water."

Marcella was lying. Max hadn't buried that bird. The ground was still frozen, and besides I saw some feathers plastered with mayonnaise sticking out of the kitchen wastebasket. Probably she did wash the plate, though.

Well, I thought, I may have lost this battle, but I still haven't lost the war. I'll get that Shadrach yet. "A little more vodka, please," I said, holding out my glass.

We were all feeling pretty good about each other again when it got to be time for me to go home. Marcella spooned some leftover chili into an old margarine container and put some more cookies on my flowered plate, covering them with foil. Then she capped the half-finished quart bottle of vodka we'd been working on. Bottle and all went into a bag for me to take home. "Fern, you and I'll go grocery shopping at the supermarket tomorrow," she promised, slurring most of her words. Marcella just can't hold her liquor.

By this time half an inch of snow had fallen, and I could see cat tracks leading toward my door. Shadrach stood right in my path, growling. I aimed a hard kick right at him. He leaped clear at the last second, and I whacked my toe on the garbage can behind him, knocking it over. It hit the pavement with a bang.

I wished I'd worn something besides my house slippers when I went out. My toes smarted something fierce from the impact. Best to get inside and numb them with some vodka.

I'll get that cat tomorrow, I swear.

Bear

"Bear, have another pancake before you leave." Susie, the trucker's wife, gestured toward the TV set. "Weather report says a big storm's moving in from the Gulf toward us. Sounds like a real bad one."

Bear Buchanan looked up from his plate. "Yeah, I'll take one more. It's a comfort to have a full stomach when there's a hard drive ahead."

"Be careful," Susie cautioned. "You know I worry about you when you're out in heavy weather."

"Hey, I'm the Bear, darlin'. I'm a tough guy who's hard to kill. I'll be just fine."

She frowned. "We're neither of us as young as we used to be."

"Well, I ain't ready for the grave yet," Bear told her. "So quit thinking about that cemetery plot your brother wants to sell us. It ain't healthy." He pushed his plate aside, stood up from the table and grabbed his wife in a bear hug. "I'll be home Wednesday night. How about making us some of your fried chicken for dinner when I get back?"

When Bear started his engine, the sky was still dark. He looked up and saw the lightning flare between the heavy clouds. Damn, the storm was moving in fast.

He pulled the heavy dump truck out onto Lake Lindsey Road and headed toward the quarry, where he'd pick up a load of crushed lime rock. He wasn't but ten miles from home, just past the Hog Island road, when the first fat drops splattered onto his windshield. Within moments, pounding rain reduced Bear's vision to mere yards.

The long slope down to the bridge that spanned the Withlacoochee River lay just ahead, and it was bound to be slippery. Bear shifted gears to slow his descent. Even so, the pale glow of the lights at the gas station flashed by faster than he would have liked. He braked cautiously to slow the truck even more as he crossed the river, and he rounded the curve on the far side without skidding. . . just barely.

Bear rolled through the hamlet of Nobleton. At this early hour, most of its inhabitants would still be half asleep, and the thunder was so loud they'd never even hear the rumble of his diesel engine. In moments he left the scattered cottages behind and entered the open country. Then he figured he was in the clear. Rain or no rain, the road here was easy for an experienced driver like him.

As he steered through the downpour, Bear concentrated on watching for the faint glow of headlights and the fainter reddish ones of taillights. Instead he saw ahead of him a darkness deeper than the storm. His gut, quicker than his mind, recognized it for a large animal emerging from the woods a few hundred feet ahead. Perhaps a feral hog, black and bristled, or a farm dog, he couldn't tell for sure. Then his unbelieving eyes took it in, a big black bear, as wild as the piney woods that grew alongside the pavement. What the hell? There weren't supposed to be any bears here, thirty miles away from their protected habitat at Chassahowitzka and even farther from either the Green Swamp or the Ocala National Forest, the only other places with room enough for the big beasts to roam. He had thought he was the only Bear in this territory.

The black bear moved at an unhurried lope, a slight hitch in its gait, as though it might have injured a paw on a thorn or perhaps a piece of broken glass encountered while foraging in the trash bins at the riverside park nearby.

It was too late to stop. Bear felt the thump as his tires rolled over the animal's heavy body. Nothing he could have done about it, he thought as he continued down the road toward the limestone quarry. He hated the idea that he'd caused the wild creature's death, but damn it all, there was no way he could have prevented it. For the rest of the day, regret haunted him, that and a tinge of fear. The bear's death had been so sudden, so unpredictable, so inevitable.

Two days later, homeward bound along Lake Lindsey Road, Bear the trucker saw a bloated mass of black fur and ripening dead flesh in the long grass near the edge of the pines.

A gang of buzzards had found the dead bear and were landing in successive waves upon the carcass, squabbling for the most tender meat.

Not even the biggest and baddest bear could live forever.

Bear the trucker took a swallow of cold coffee from his Thermos and wondered idly if he and Susie should write a check for that funeral plot.

Then he remembered that he'd soon be home, and Susie would have fried chicken and biscuits ready for him.

He was Bear, and he was a tough man, hard to kill. Mortality was for wimps.

Why I Am Late

The alarm clock went off at 8 AM sharp. Damn! I was sure I had set it for 7. I barely had time to shave, get dressed and get to work. Wouldn't you know it—we had a meeting with a big-bucks prospective client, and I had the only key to the conference room. I know, I was supposed to leave it with the receptionist yesterday, after I'd gotten the room set up for the meeting, but by the time I remembered that, she'd locked her desk drawer and gone home for the day. Damned clock-watching witch! You get the picture—I just had to be at the office on time today.

But that's not why I'm Late. Actually, I am the third guy in my family to be Late. Yep, it's a family name. I'm Late R. Jenkins, with three Roman number ones after my last name.

As I turned on the bathroom light, the bulb flashed bright and then died. I uttered a stream of profanities and went to find a new bulb. Oops. They'd been on my grocery list for weeks, but I'd never gotten around to buying them. No bulbs. I stumped out to my work shed to retrieve the utility light. I said a prayer and plugged it in. It worked. There wasn't anything in the bathroom to hang it on, though. I draped it over an open cabinet door and plastered shaving cream on my face just as the utility light slid off the cabinet door and hit the marble tile flooring. Crash! No more utility light. Guess I wasn't supposed to shave this morning. I rinsed off the shaving cream and ran a brush through my hair before sweeping up the shards of glass. A glance at the bedroom clock told me it was 8:10. I had to be at work at nine.

But that's not why I'm late.

I scrounged up a clean shirt and a tie. Where were my trousers? Oh, yeah, I'd managed to pick up my dry cleaning after work yesterday—just moments before the shop closed. I tore open the plastic envelope over the newly cleaned clothes and took out a pair of slacks. I had them almost all the way on before I discovered I was trying to put both of my legs into a single pants leg. There was almost room in there, too. This pair of trousers would have fit my 400 pound uncle—they were definitely not MY pants.

But now I was stuck in that pants leg. I started hopping around, trying to get one foot free, and I lost my balance. Whack! My forehead met the bed-post at high speed. When I woke up again, I eyed the clock from my position on the bedroom floor. Uh-oh. Almost 8:20. I squirmed out of the outsize pants before I tried to get up again and then put on the trousers I'd been wearing for the last couple of days. There was a ketchup stain on them from yesterday's burger. It went nicely with the splotch of yellow mustard from the day before, not to mention the purple hue beginning to suffuse my right eye. But at least the conference room key was in the pocket.

But that's not why I'm late.

There was just enough time before I had to leave to make myself a slice of toast. I popped a piece of bread into my brand-new toaster and got the butter out of the fridge. There was a whirr and a sprong, and my toast flew across the counter and fell into the sink, landing in a bowlful of dirty water, which splattered all over my clean shirt—my only clean shirt. Back to the closet for a sweater vest that would cover the damage. Never mind that the day promised to reach 100 in the shade. And it was now 8:30.

But that's not why I'm late.

I snatched up my car keys and stepped out the front door, only to trip over a plump armadillo. I landed face down in the pile of sand it had just dug up. The armadillo glared at me, looking down its leprous nose, and then ducked into the brush. I swear it was laughing. I sneezed out a snootful of sand and hunted for a handkerchief, a piece of Kleenex or even a sheet of newspaper from the bottom of a birdcage. Nothing doing. I wiped my nose on my sleeve and opened up the car. It was now 8:35.

If I really put the pedal to the metal, I might just make it.

But that's not why I'm late.

Two miles from the office, the car bucked and jerked, sputtering. I looked at the gas gauge. Empty. Luckily I'd stalled just outside a gas station. I ran in, negotiated for a new gas can and filled it up. By now I was really getting panicked. I opened the gas cap with shaking hands. To calm my nerves, I took a cigarette from the pack in my shirt pocket and searched for my lighter. Not there. Good thing — in that moment, I realized I might have blown myself up.

But that's not why I'm late.

It was now 8:45. I leaped into the car, started it and floored it, blowing through several red lights to the tune of dozens of honking horns. I pulled into the parking lot at precisely 8:55 and bolted for the elevator. I think I left the car running. But I was lucky — the elevator was on the first floor, doors open. I ran in and punched floor 25. Swoosh! Up I went. The elevator opened. I darted out and yanked on the double glass doors to the office. What? Locked? And there were no lights on. Well, then, if nobody was here, then I must not be late after all. Woo hoo!

Just then a janitor came down the hall, trundling his cleaning bucket and a mop alongside him.

"Hey, buddy," he yelled. "Whaddaya think you're doin' here?"

"I work here, dammit. And I've got a meeting in what — 30 seconds. I can't afford to be late."

The janitor laughed, a short snide chuckle. "It's Saturday, pal. Ain't nobody gonna be comin' to work today 'ceptin us janitors."

Shit. I spun around. The elevator doors were still open, and I stalked angrily in. Whoa! There wasn't anything there, nothing but cables flashing by my disbelieving eyes and a long dark abyss where the elevator floor should have been.

And that, dear people, is why I am speaking to you via this seance — and that is why I am the late Late R. Jenkins the Third.

heroes & villains

The magician Merlin had a strange laugh, and it was heard when nobody else was laughing...
He laughed because he knew what was coming next.

— Robertson Davies

The Heir of Dun Eistean

Flames roared up the ancient walls of Dun Carloway, devouring the timbers within. Even with his
hands pressed hard over his ears, Coinneach
Moireasdan could hear the hoarse screams of the
men trapped inside the tower, roasting within their
steel cuirasses. Hardened warriors every one, they
would gladly have fought to their deaths in honest
battle. But to die this way, imprisoned behind iron-
bound gates, the swords in their strong hands useless against the massed MacAulay clansmen outside–to die this way–the very sky should weep in
witness to their fate.

Old Coinneach moaned, powerless to help, as the greedy blaze devoured the flower of the Moireasdans, melting their flesh, vaporizing their blood, boiling the marrow in their shattering bones. He wept futile tears, knowing their moisture could not quench the flames.

Then, with the stench of burning meat in his nostrils, he awakened to the cries of the circling gulls.

Bewildered, the old man blinked, trying to clear his eyes. He wondered for a moment how it was that he was still alive. Why had he not burned to death along with his sons and the sons of his sons? Then the wind shifted, and he tasted the salt breeze off the ocean, the taste of home, long miles north of Dun Carloway. He found himself hunched on a flat stone in front of his turf hut, staring at the burnt remains of his intended dinner. He must have dozed off after he had set the cauldron on the fire. Along with broth and onions, there had been a few scraps of good mutton in it, given to him by the people of the village. The god knew the villagers had little enough to eat, but they had spared some for him. Now nothing remained in the pot but inedible shreds of charred meat. The smell of it sickened him.

Coinneach would make his meal of dried fish instead–hardly a sacrifice after what he had just witnessed. For he knew that the fiery massacre he had just witnessed was no mere dream. It was a true vision that the god had granted him–not the new god that had come to the Isles with Padraig of Ireland but Lugh of the Long Arm, Coinneach's own patron.

The old druid arose with difficulty, his knees and his hips aching. This cold isle, Leodhas, was no friend to old men. Yet Coinneach would live no-where else. The Moireasdans, descended from Picts, Scots and Vikings, had lived on its rugged shores as far back as druidic memory could recall–and that was a very long time. He turned toward the hut, where strips of cod hung from driftwood racks, dry-ing in the salt air. On the hill behind it, stark against the cloudless blue sky, stood the remains of an an-cient fortress, a few tumbled stone walls and a dis-integrating keep. Dun Eistean it was called, the one-time stronghold of the Moireasdans. Coinneach had once hoped to see it restored, but after this day, no one was left to rebuild it. His sons and his nephews and their sons too–gone, incinerated by the MacAu-lays, damn them.

Coinneach considered joining them in death. A single step from the cliffs where he sat and he would plunge to the pitiless rocks below. But no, that way was closed to him until–well, he didn't know what he awaited, only that he must wait. Once he had known. He shook his grizzled head and pulled a strip of dried cod from the rack, gnawing at it with his few remaining teeth. Old men who must wait must also eat.

After Coinneach's vision of fire, the ravens vis-ited him more often. They spoke to him, but he had forgotten their language. He had known so much, once. Perhaps in his youth, at the peak of his Druidic powers, he might have saved the men. Perhaps not. The gods bestowed and withdrew their gifts at their whims. The old man had done as the god Lugh de-manded. He had taught the arcane knowledge to the youngest son of his youngest son. That done, he had forgotten almost all the lore his own grandfather had instilled in him. That was the way of the power, demanding to be passed on. Surely now, with the men of the clan cravenly murdered, the power was lost for good.

Once or twice a week, the women of the Moireasdan clan trudged up the long hill from their tumbledown village to Coinneach's clifftop hut. They brought him scones baked in the ashes of their fires. He wondered where they found enough barley to make them. The fields had lain uncultivated since the men had gone to war. Sometimes the women brought him an onion or two, or a turnip. They came, their eyes full of the question they feared to ask: When would their men come home?

He could not bear to tell them:

Never.

Summer faded into a brief autumn. The old man knew winter had come when the windblown sea spray crystallized to ice upon the fallen stones of Dun Eistean. Then he retreated to the shell of the ruined keep, where the walls remained sound enough to keep out the wind. There, with driftwood and turves, he had roofed over a nook where he could sleep protected from the cold rains. Lovely Seonag, his grandson's wife, was the only one who came to him then, making sure he had warm blankets to ward his old bones from the cold.

Seonag was an uncanny sort, with hair so pale it shone silver in the sunlight and long uptilted eyes, green as the sweet grass of the machair turf. Young Donnchadh Moireasdan, a skillful sailor, had fetched her from the mainland–so he had said. But old Coinneach had recognized that she had come from that other place, the one that lay near and yet so very far from the world in which humans resided.

Like the old man, Seonag waited and watched. Daily her belly grew larger. Coinneach counted the days and knew that her time would come soon. He sensed her thought: If only her husband would return. Yet Coinneach held out no hope that young Donnchadh, the son of his son, might have survived.

And then, on the longest and darkest day of the winter, as she sat with the old druid, Seonag cried out with such anguish that the remaining stones of Dun Eistean should have crumbled. She leaped up, staring at her ring on her right hand. Coinneach knew that ring, a huge transparent blue stone set in silver. His grandson Donnchadh wore one like it. The old man recognized the rings as the work of faery. With their matched rings, the white maiden, Seonag, and the young Druid, Donnchadh, had plighted their troth.

The light had faded from Seonag's stone, its sapphire brilliance dimmed to the gray of the winter waves.

Coinneach could offer her no comfort.

Tears spilling from her eyes, Seonag turned to him. "Grandfather, I must see my Donnchadh once more before he departs from this world," she said. "Forgive me for leaving you all alone here." From the leather purse she wore at her belt she pulled out a small white packet. Holding it by one corner, she shook it, opening it out into a cloak of snowy white feathers.

For a moment the old man sat stunned into silence. Seonag had known that Donnchadh Moireasdan had not perished in the flaming tower.

She had known that her husband lived. She knew that now her husband was in dire peril. That was the message of the ring.

"If you put that cloak on, you might find him, but you will never return to his bed," warned the old druid. For he understood what she meant to do, and he foresaw the result.

"If I do not, I shall never see him again, in this life or any other." She embraced the old man, her tears dampening his weathered cheeks. Releasing him, she wrapped the feathery cloak around her shoulders, and then she was gone. Through eyes rheumy and weak with age, Coinneach thought he discerned a swan soar far, far off in the milky sky.

When Seonag vanished, the aged druid left the shelter he had built in the ruined keep and walked out into the blustery cold. He scarcely felt it even though it soon penetrated his ragged garments. Gazing out over the heaving gray sea, he remembered a spell that his grandfather had passed down to him. It was not one to trifle with. Yet, if his grandson still lived, the spell could buy the young man's life. Coinneach chanted as he paced the clifftops.

In the village below the druid's clifftop eyrie, the forsaken wives and mothers glimpsed what the old wizard had conjured: a gigantic female figure cloaked in shadows. The women smothered their cookfires and put out their rushlights, lest they call attention to themselves. Huddling together, they made the sign of the cross and mouthed prayers to the new god of the isles, for they knew and feared that apparition: the Morrigan, the black one, the chooser of the slain.

At last the winter storms blew over. On the spring morning that the solitary rider approached Dun Eistean, a brittle sun had risen in a cold sky. Coinneach watched as the rider dismounted, tethering the horse to a stone in the meadow below the keep. The old man squinted, the better to see. The newcomer, wrapped in a wool plaid of faded red, staggered and almost fell when he released his hold on the animal. He caught himself, one hand clutching at his chest, and stumbled toward the druid's hut.

As the rider came closer, Coinneach registered the man's ruddy hair and beard, much like his own ha been when he had been a young. He saw the warrior's red surcoat, darkened with dried blood, and he saw the shattered remains of a mail byrnie poking through the rents in the surcoat. Then he knew that this was what he had been waiting for so many empty days: the return of Donnchadh, his beloved grandson.

The warrior unbuckled the baldric that held his claymore and set the weapon aside. "Grandfather," he said, and he embraced the old man in arms not as strong as they should have been.

"Donnchadh, son of my son," said the old man. "I am glad beyond measure to see you. What news do you bring?"

"None of it good. The Moireasdans are no more," replied the younger one. "Burned, all but me, by the men of Clan MacAulay."

"This much have I seen in visions," the old one said. "But you are alive."

"Very soon I too shall join the fallen. Grandfather, I was riding among the men of Clan MacLeod on the day our warriors burned to death, so I was spared their fate. Oh, I made Clan MacAulay pay dearly for the death of the Moireasdan men. I fought shoulder to shoulder with the MacLeods in the battle that finally destroyed our common enemy, and my blade cut down many a MacAulay clansman. But they wounded me gravely. I have survived this long only that I might come home to say farewell to my dearest Seonag."

The old druid turned his face away from Donnchadh. "Seonag is not here," he said.

"She has forsaken me? How can that be? I loved her with all that I was, and she–she abandoned her folk for love of me. Where has she gone?"

"I do not know," the old man said softly. "She waited for your return, oh, so long, long after the burning of Dun Carloway. I could not tell her your fate, though the god knows I tried to scry you in my silver bowl, in my polished crystal sphere, in the smoke from the sacred fire. My arts went for naught. But Seonag had more faith than I, and she waited. Then only a fortnight ago she looked at the ring she wore upon her right hand, and she began to weep. When she had cried her last tear–hours later, it seemed to me–she donned a cloak of white feathers– oh, yes, lad, I know what kind of bride you had wed, for long ago an otherwordly seal maiden loved me. No good comes of it when such beings–swan maidens or seal maidens–steal the heart of a mortal man."

Coinneach paused a moment, remembering. Then he resumed. "Seonag told me that she must find you, to see you for the last time in this mortal realm. I could not stop her. I could only watch as she beat her wings, flinging herself into the sky. Soon she was lost to my sight, and she has not returned. I fear she is lost to you."

"But look, grandfather!" The young man extended his scarred right hand, displaying a silver ring set with a single sapphire, large and lustrous, upon his third finger. "The stone in my ring is unchanged. It's still as bright and blue as the summer sky. Wherever my Seonag has gone, she is well."

"And what of the stone in the ring she wears upon her own right hand? I saw it myself, its stone dark as death."

Old Coinneach could see the effort of will that Donnchadh Moireasdan exerted to quell the pain of his wounded body and his stricken heart. He reached out and took the hand with the ring into his own right hand, waiting until the young man had steadied himself. When at last Donnchadh did speak, sorrow infused his voice. "Grandfather, if my lady is not here, she and I will not meet again in this life. Look you there–already the ravens watch from atop the old keep of Dun Eistean, eager to feast upon the flesh I must soon abandon."

The old man spoke slowly, his voice low and powerful. The winds that swirled around the pair carried the sound to the tower and beyond, to the skies. "The ravens await someone else. You are the designated heir of Dun Eistean. In the Moireasdans reside the mysteries and the laws of Leodhas. The god Lugh has decreed that we must carry it on, from generation to generation. As my grandfather trained me in its precepts, so have I taught you. In turn, you may not die until you have brought up a grandchild of your blood in the secret lore. You will live until you pass the stewardship of the Moireasdans to one of our own."

Coinneach know how empty the words must sound to the bereaved warrior. Yet they were true. Inescapably, implacably true.

The younger man gestured toward the ruined tower. "Heir to what? The stronghold, grandfather? Look at the fallen walls, the roofless keep. Like me, Dun Eistean is wounded unto death, and none shall rebuild it, for few Moireasdans survive to care. The druid lore? A new god has come to our isle. That one has no use for our knowledge."

"In the eyes of Lugh, the new god of the isles signifies nothing," stated the old druid.

"As for me," Donnchadh continued as though his grandfather had not spoken, "the Morrigan, that black goddess of death, has chosen me for her bridegroom. See, there she stands, upon the ruined tower, waiting to enfold me in her black cloak. I may not deny her."

"Listen, my beloved warrior," Coinneach said. "The tower does not matter. It is what the old keep means, the stewardship of the ancient and sacred lore that you are destined to uphold. As I have trained you, you must raise up a grandson and teach him. Else all the clans of Leodhas–the MacLeods, the MacDonalds, the MacAskills, the MacKenzies, the others–will see their glory fade, the prowess of their men extinguished, their descendants reduced to poverty of mind and body."

"Tell that to the ravens," Donnchadh said. His voice betrayed his growing weakness.

"Ah, and I have," said his grandsire. "I have waited so long in Dun Eistean that death and I have become old friends." He paused, reaching out to touch the young man's shoulder. "Now, son of my son, turn your face away from me and look to the south. Something comes. My eyes have grown dull with age. I cannot be sure what I see. Tell me."

Donnchadh turned a strained and bloodless face in the direction his grandfather indicated. From his seat on the high cliffs his keen eyes, as yet undimmed by approaching death, gazed into the azure distance, where flecks of white appeared in the crystalline sky. "Terns, perhaps, or gulls," he said, "though I have never seen the sea birds fly with such purpose. Nay, they cannot be gulls, though they are white."

On the tower, the Morrigan's ravens croaked a hungry complaint.

"No, not gulls," he repeated. "Swans? Could they be? I count five, soaring strong. A sixth one flies low, as though carrying a heavy weight."

"I see them now," said the old man. "They are seeking you."

"The swan maidens? Seonag?" asked the younger. "But if she were among them, there would be seven swans."

The swans neared. They circled the ruined tower and alighted in the meadow near Donnchadh Moireasdan's grazing horse. The stallion lifted his head and whinnied as though in greeting.

Then the swans vanished and in their place stood six willowy maidens clad in white silk, with white plumes bound into their long silver hair. One bore an infant in each arm. Stepping away from the others, she walked toward the seated men.

"My sisters," said the young warrior. "My sisters, have you brought news of Seonag?"

"I have brought you these, your lady's son and daughter," the maiden answered. "Your son and your daughter. Our beloved sister Seonag flew out in search of you. She was pregnant, too heavy to fly high above the earth. She made a compelling target for a starving man's bow. In her anguish, Seonag called out to us. We came and carried her to a safe place, where she gave birth. She made us promise to bring her babes to their father."

"But her ring–her ring shows no blemish!" protested Donnchadh, holding out his hand for them to see. "She cannot be dead!"

"Look to the sky," replied the swan maiden.

Old Coinneach's head lifted in unison with his grandson's. High above them the seventh swan circled, her wingbeats full of grace.

"Her mortal form has died," continued the swan maiden. "The woman you knew as Seonag, the wife you loved, has returned to the other world as a swan, and there she is immortal. But she cannot rejoin you, and she grieves her loss as you must grieve yours. For she loves you still."

Donnchadh summoned the strength to stand, but only momentarily. He cried out his lady's name and then fell senseless to the earth.

Coinneach leaped up from his stone seat like a young man. Turning, he railed at the Morrigan, accusing the goddess of deceit as though she were nothing more than a village woman trying to pass off yesterday's bread as fresh. "My life for his," he shouted. "That was our bargain. Even you, black one, must honor it, in the name of Lugh of the Long Arm."

"And so I shall," came the reply, in a voice that struck Coinneach through the heart like his god's golden spear.

"Then restore the mother of his children to him," the old druid demanded.

"That I cannot. It is not granted me to interfere with the fate of immortals, and Seonag is an immortal being." The Morrigan's midnight robe swirled about her as she glided toward him, her right hand extended. He had thought it meant for him, to take him, but instead she reached down to stroke the forehead of the dying warrior. "I keep my bargain. Your grandson will live. I did not promise you that he would enjoy happiness."

In front of the fallen Donnchadh, the Morrigan stood watching. Behind him, the swan maidens waited. Beside him, Coinneach grieved silently. On the ground, the young man stirred, his chest rising and falling with renewed breath. Slowly he sat up, color returning to his face.

"I live," he said softly. "O Morrigan, I am yours. Why do I yet live?" He read the answer in the dark, stern face. "Ah, I see. A life for a life. My lady's for mine."

"Nay," his grandfather said. "My life, for yours. That was the bargain I chose. Seonag was mistress of her own fate. Now, dear warrior, stand and take your bairns into your arms."

The swan maiden who held the babes spoke. "Donnchadh, your beloved Seonag bade me tell you this: Here are your children, your gallant young

Cailean and your bonny Lillias, begotten of the love she shared with you."

Donnchadh took the girl child first, then the boy.

"While you have them, your love is not lost," said the swan maiden.

"You must teach them the laws of man as you were taught," said Coinneach, old druid that he was, "that Clan Moireasdan may yet prosper."

"Seonag!" Donnchadh cried to the skies. "You ask too much, that I must live without you!"

"For her sake, you must live and care for the bairns," said the silvery maiden. She and her sisters faded, and where they had stood six swans stretched their great wings and lifted into the sky. The seventh swan, she who had circled above them, swooped close to earth. A wing tip brushed Donnchadh's cheek. A white plume drifted into the baby Cailean's grasp. Cooing, the boychild clutched it firmly. From the bird's bill dropped a golden whistle. It fell into the white linen swaddling that enfolded wee Lillias. Donnchadh heard his lady's voice whisper in the wind, "Keep my plume and my whistle in memory of me. When death summons you, take up the whistle and breathe my name into it. Do as I ask, and happiness may yet be ours."

And then the swans were gone.

"Promise me that you will care for your bairns," old Coinneach said.

Donnchadh bent his face to the babies. His tears dropped upon Lillias' tiny features. The infant opened eyes as green as her mother's. "So, little ones, my lady lives on in you."

When he raised his head again, it was to face Coinneach a final time. "I do promise, grandfather, that I will love them and care for them. For Seonag's sake and for yours."

"I am content. Leave me now, Donnchadh. Saddle your horse and set the babes upon him. In the village below, you'll find a young woman who has recently lost her child. She will suckle your son and your daughter."

"When I go, how will it be with you, grandfather?"

"My work is done. Because you and your children live, the heritage of the Moireasdan druids will endure after me. My death is upon me, and I welcome it like an old friend."

"Lugh be with you, then," said the young man.

Wrapping his infant twins in his worn plaid, Donnchadh laid them on the soft grass. With renewed vitality, he slung his baldric and sword across his back and retrieved his saddle and bridle. Without being called, the stallion trotted across the lush grass to his master's side. Donnchadh strapped the saddle onto the patient animal. Placing the swaddled bairns upon it, he strode off toward the village. He did not look back.

Old Coinneach turned toward the Morrigan. "Is it time?" he asked.

"It is," said she of the midnight cloak.

Sitting down upon the rock once more, the old man extracted a silver whistle from the pouch at his belt. Many a lonely night he had held it in his hands. But never had he played upon it, for the time had not yet come. Now, taking a deep breath and raising it to his lips, he piped an uncanny song made up of bird calls, wind whistling among the rocks and the hiss of breaking waves.

Something filmy and vague drifted up from the sea and came to stand before him. An observer, if there had been one, might have thought the form to be a seal. And then it changed into a woman, ageless and fair. She took the old man by the hand and bade him arise. Young, strong, handsome, Coinneach Moireasdan obeyed. The Morrigan wrapped her cloak of shadows around the pair, bearing them from the sight of living men.

The careworn flesh that had housed the old druid's spirit collapsed among the fallen stones of Dun Eistean.

Their hunger great, the ravens spread their wings and flapped down from the ruined tower to partake of their long-awaited meal.

Dramatis Personae
In Order of Appearance

Coinneach Moireasdan (Scots Gaelic: translates into English as Kenneth Morrison): a Druid in the service of the ancient Celtic god, Lugh (pronounced like Hugh) of the Long Arm

Seonag Moireasdan (Scots Gaelic: translates into English as Joan Morrison : wife of Donnchadh (Duncan) Moireasdan

Donnchadh Moireasdan: (Scots Gaelic: translates into English as Duncan Morrison): grandson of Coinneach Moireasdan

Padraig of Ireland: St. Patrick, missionary to the Irish and Scottish Gaels)

Lugh of the Long Arm (pronounced like Hugh): a Celtic sky god. The "long arm" is his golden spear, which is believed to represent lightning.

Cailean Moireasdan (Scots Gaelic: translates into English as Colin Morrison): infant son of Seonag and Donnchadh Moireasdan

Lillias Moireasdan (Scots Gaelic: translates into English as Lillie or Lily Morrison): infant daughter of Seonag and Donnchadh Moireasdan

Note: Dun Eistean (Hugh's Fort) is the ancient fortress of Clan Moireasdan (Morrison). Pronounced Dun Ashden, Dun Eistean is located at the far northern tip of the Isle of Leodhas (Lewis) in the Outer Hebrides of Scotland.

Two Crows Discover
the Meaning of Chivalry

The knight sprawled in the long grass beside the ancient dyke, blood crusting on his armor. His dented helmet lay on the far side of the meadow, where the hooves of heavy war horses had gouged deep furrows into the unresisting earth. The scabbard belted at his side angled between his legs, as though to trip him. The hilt of a sword poked out from under his back. The breeze had caught the long locks of his fair hair and flung them across his face, veiling his pale features.

High overhead, sharp eyes marked the fallen man–eyes familiar with battlefields and the feasts that awaited when the living men had gone and only the dead remained. It had been a brief battle–two men on horseback meeting by accident in this remote place, one a stranger, one a minor lord abiding in what passed locally for a manor. One with a finer horse, reason enough to fight. The other with a lady riding pillion behind him. When a man hadn't lain with a woman for a very long time, she served as another compelling reason to fight.

The screams of the woman, the rattle and clang of sword against armor and the whinnies of the horses alerted the birds, which had been lazily circling the skies, looking for meat, preferably not too decomposed, for their daily meal. Perhaps, if they were lucky, they would feast this day on human flesh.

Soon enough the men had unhorsed each other and fought blade to blade, while the woman watched, fist to mouth to stop her screams. The horses wandered away from the warriors and began snatching up mouthfuls of the sweet grass.

Then one man fell and did not rise again.

The man still standing turned toward the woman, sword in hand. She was a thin waif clad in a shapeless homespun tunic, not a lady at all, only some peasant girl. But she would do. He offered a mock bow as he bent to wipe his sword on the grass, and then grabbed her by the arm. "If I didn't have this armor on, I'd–come with me, woman." She offered no resistance as he shoved her up onto the nearer horse. The second animal, the finer one, reared up at his approach, hooves threatening to strike. No matter. He had the woman. Awkward in his armor, he clambered into the saddle and kicked the horse's side. The animal moved off at a trot that shook the ground. The crows noted the man's departure.

How long must a hungry bird wait for a meal spread before it? The glittering eyes in the crows' dark heads eyed the motionless body below. They circled lower. They had encountered armor before, and they knew their beaks lacked power to peck through it. But an errant gust of wind lifted the tangled hair, baring the soft tissues of the dead man's neck. There –

The bolder of the two crows flew close, snatching a hank of the man's the golden hair. 'Twould line and soften the nest for the chicks when they emerged from their eggs. The second bird followed suit, pulling out a beakful of the silken strands. The man did not stir. The birds made for their nest.

And returned.

The first crow discovered a slash high on the man's unarmored thigh and lifted its beak to peck at the bloody flesh. The second, heavy with eggs, landed upon the steel breastplate and eyed the meat of the neck. The skin would be soft there, easy to tear. She cocked her head, looking for the most likely spot.

And found a fist closing around her neck. Her astonished caw broke off as the hand tightened. A blue eye full of death stared at her.

"Two crows, is it now," grumbled the man. "Hoping to eat me, eh? Too bad for you. I was just resting here. I was all tired out from that fight. I don't intend to become a meal for a couple of misbegotten scavengers. Now that I think of it, I'm hungry. One of you would do for an appetizer."

"Wait, this is not how the story is supposed to end," said the second crow.

"Oh, you can speak?" said the man. "Then you must be birds of the gods. What divine reward will you give me if I spare your lives?"

"We are only crows," said the first bird. "We are not Odin's ravens, not even messenger birds. Just hungry crows. Look, my lady is heavy with our eggs. Would you kill her now, just before our young are born?"

"Why should I not? Already she has pulled out some of my hair. She would have pecked out my eyes next. And then eaten my liver."

"We thought you were dead."

"So, I suppose, did I," said the knight. "But as you see, I am not, and as your bad luck would have it, soon you shall be."

He tightened his grip on the female crow. Her eyes bulged in her black head. Then he relented, but only a trifle.

"Dear my love, save me," she croaked.

"What must we do?" asked her mate.

"Bring back my wench," said the man. "And my hawk, and my hound."

"You had only the wench," replied the crow. "Not those other creatures. We saw. We cannot give you what you never had."

"So you can give me something, though. Then bring me the girl, for she can tend my wounds."

"It shall be so," said the crow. "Only let my dear one live."

And off he flew.

Once the male crow had soared out of sight, the knight sat up, held the female in both hands, and twisted its neck until the tiny bones snapped. He threw the body aside.

He heard the stamp of hooves, the ringing of the bridle. The man astride the horse shoved the woman off. She fell to the ground but got up and came running toward the seated knight, but the crow reached him first, shrieking, "Liar! Murderer!"

The dishonorable man smiled at the wench–but only for as long as it took for her captor to lean down from his cantering horse, swinging his sword and severing the liar's head cleanly from his oh-so-succulent neck.

The rider seized the woman again and tossed her across his horse's withers.

Well satisfied with the outcome, the remaining crow landed upon the dead man's breast. He could always find another mate, but good meals were hard to come by.

Lynx in a Chain

"This road leads straight to heaven, Barry," Gabe Conforti announced as he powered his Ford Expedition up the steep grade toward the alpine meadows of Wyoming's Big Horn Mountains. "Have you ever seen anything so magnificent?" He gestured toward the snowy peaks towering above.

Gabe had been my best friend since we both landed jobs at the same Chicago law firm. We were unlikely pals. Gabe's parents owned several sporting goods stores in Colorado. He and his two younger sisters had enjoyed many a camping trip.

No comfy RVs for them–Spartan tents and back-packs instead. Gabe loved hiking, hunting and fishing above all things.

I was an only child, named Barrett Cahill after my grandfather. My dad scripted commercials for an advertising agency, and my mom taught fiber arts at the Art Institute of Chicago. Our family trips centered around visits to museums and libraries. My pursuit of outdoor sports was limited to dining al fresco at sidewalk cafés and attending summer concerts in the Grant Park bandshell with Lexi, my fiancee.

But Gabe and I shared a powerful interest in criminal law and dedication to physical fitness. Lean and wiry, Gabe was determined to keep in shape for his wilderness adventures. I'm tall and big-boned, gifted with a physique that helps me project an intimidating presence in the courtroom. Gabe and I paired up for thrice-weekly workouts at the gym.

Gabe didn't wait for me to answer his questions. He continued expounding. "Everything a man could possibly want is up here, incredible scenery, good fishing and absolute solitude. No wife and kids to chain you up."

"Speaking of wives, what about Amy?" I asked him. He'd been sharing an apartment with Amy Sanders, a court reporter and a real knockout babe, for at least a year. "Isn't it about time the two of you tied the knot?"

"No way! She knows I'm not interested in marriage. I told her if her biological clock is ticking that fast, she'd be better off with someone else."

"Idiot," I muttered under my breath. I might have told Gabe that Amy was the best thing that was ever likely to happen to him, but I had developed a headache that was short-circuiting my synapses. I rubbed my temples with both hands.

Gabe glanced at me. "Looks like you're starting to feel the effects of the altitude, Barry. It's nothing to fret about. You're in good shape, and you'll soon get used to these heights."

Easy for him to say. I'd suspected from the get-go that accompanying Gabe on this expedition might not be the smartest thing I'd ever done. But with my wedding to Lexi just a few weeks away, Gabe had decided it was his masculine duty to initiate me into the glories of the wilderness. "Soon, my urbane friend, you'll be permanently grounded by married life," he'd said. "It's now or never."

Despite my misgivings, I accepted his invitation. We loaded Gabe's Expedition with camping gear and drove to Sheridan, Wyoming, where we abandoned the paved highways in favor of this gravel road leading to the back of beyond.

Gabe and I were watching the road ahead for potholes when a flash of spotted fur sprang out of the brush and leaped across the road just in front of our SUV, startling us both.

"My God, what's that?" I exclaimed.

"A lynx!" Gabe hit the brakes, hoping for a better look, but the animal had already vanished into the timber. "A real, honest-to-God lynx! I've never seen one in the wild before."

I knew Gabe well enough that I could almost hear his thoughts. He imagined himself to be like that cat, at home in the wilderness, solitary by choice, needing only his own strength and cunning. I knew he thought of me as something resembling a

well-trained Great Dane, big and strong but still domesticated, bound to a pack consisting of office col-
leagues, relatives and my bride-to-be. His attitude
pissed me off, but I kept my mouth shut.

The moment over, Gabe punched the accelera-
tor. The SUV jolted up several more miles of rough
road to the alpine meadow where the trail began.
The only other vehicle there was the trail hosts'
camper. We parked next to the camper and un-
loaded our gear.

"Do we camp here tonight?" I was hoping for a
chance to lie down and close my eyes until my head
quit aching.

"Hell, no. We've still got a couple of hours of
daylight left. Let's not waste them." So we shoul-
dered our packs and hiked into the pines until we
found a grassy clearing a few miles beyond the trailhead.

Instructing me to set up our tent, Gabe went off
to gather wood for a campfire. I pulled the tent out
of its stuff sack, unfurled it, and tried to make sense
out of the folds of green ripstop nylon and a jumble
of tent poles. When Gabe returned with an armload
of branches, I was still trying to figure out which tent
poles should be inserted into which tent casings.

"Whoa!" Gabe realized I had no idea what to do
next. He dropped his stack of firewood next to the
stone fire ring and sighed. "Dammit, Barry, I
thought you knew how to put up a tent."

I'd had only one lesson in setting up a tent,
when the salesman at the sporting goods store had
demonstrated how easy it was. I could feel the burn
as my face turned red.

"Look here." Gabe shook one of the poles in my face. "This pole, this long one, goes diagonally across the tent itself. It gives the tent its shape. The second long pole goes at right angles to the first..." He continued to explain the procedure while I followed his instructions, fuming all the while.

"Do you think you can build a fire?" Gabe asked. I felt the condescension in his voice. "Once we hit the trail, it'll be mostly freeze-dried meals, but tonight we're going to enjoy steaks and toast our mountain vacation with a good Cabernet I brought."

Trying to recall how we did it when I was a twelve-year old at Boy Scout camp, I started stacking the biggest logs in the fire ring.

Gabe sighed again. "Barry, don't you know those big logs won't burn right away." He held up a handful of dry twigs and pine needles. "This is tinder. It burns quick and hot. So you start with tinder and then add kindling–these smaller branches."

I bit my tongue before I said something I'd regret.

"Now light the tinder." Gabe handed me a box of wind-resistant matches. Wind-resistant or not, it took me three tries to ignite the tinder. But at last the fire blazed, burning the logs down into glowing coals perfect for grilling our steaks. Angry as I was, I have to admit I enjoyed that meal.

Early the next morning, Gabe unzipped the tent's front door, sticking his head out to test the weather. "Brrrr! It's colder than it has any right to be for July, even here in the Big Horns. Let's get that fire going."

It took me only moments to light the fire this time. As soon as it was blazing, we set the saucepans full of water over it, shivering as we waited for it to boil. Breakfast was instant oatmeal and instant coffee.

As we stepped off again, Gabe pointed toward the high peaks. "The trout are up there waiting for us to come and tease them onto our hooks. You've never eaten anything as fine as a fat trout you've caught yourself and cooked over a campfire."

Gabe took the lead, striding confidently along the trail until it joined a rutted dirt road. At the junction stood a rustic wooden sign carved with the words "Twin Spears" and an arrow pointed in the direction we were headed.

"Twin Spears? What the devil is that?" I wondered.

"It's a dude ranch, kind of fancy for back here," explained Gabe. "They've actually got an airstrip for rich guys who don't want to risk their Beemers on the road we drove up. You'll see."

Sure enough, we soon reached a ranch-style gate topped with another carved wooden sign identifying the place as Twin Spears. Gabe opened the gate, motioned for me to pass through and closed the gate behind us.

"Aren't we trespassing?

"No, the trail crosses the ranch lands here. The National Forest Service has a special dispensation. Hikers are welcome to stop at the lodge for a coffee break or even a meal."

A few bucks bought us mugs of steaming coffee, a plateful of buttery cinnamon rolls and the company of several wranglers who'd just finished saddling up the horses for the guests' morning trail ride.

"Where you boys headed?" the wranglers wanted to know. Gabe named a destination that meant nothing to me.

"Been a lot of snow up high this year, and the meltwater's still flowing down," offered one of the ranch hands, a weathered older guy who introduced himself as Steve Mitchell. "The rivers are overflowing with fast water. I wouldn't try to ford them on foot, if I were you."

Gabe swallowed the last of his coffee. "I'm not worried. I've been up here before during high water season."

"This is the worst I've seen in years," warned Mitchell. "There's plenty of good fishing on the lower slopes."

"Thanks for the advice." Gabe rose and hefted his pack. "We'll be careful."

"Nice canteen you're carrying," Mitchell commented. "I haven't seen one like it in years. Good solid metal and that thick red plaid flannel on the outside. A little heavy for backpacking, though."

"My grandfather gave it to me years ago," Gabe explained. "I like it better than the new plastic bottles, and I don't mind a bit of extra weight. Besides, it kinda feels like a good luck charm."

We hit the trail again, climbing uphill until late afternoon. I had thought I was fit, but I found myself tiring easily and requested what I thought was an occasional break to snack on a protein bar. But Gabe got annoyed with my frequent requests for breaks. "We're not making the distance I'd hoped for," he complained. "But I guess it wasn't fair to ask a deskbound intellectual like you to become a mountain hiker overnight."

"Damn straight it wasn't," I snapped back. His tally of my inadequacies was getting to me. "I never pretended to be one. But remember this the next time you ask me to spot you when you're trying to bench a couple hundred pounds–less than half of what I lift–then you'll know who's the tough guy."

Still, I was determined to prove I could be as much of an outdoorsman as Gabe. I quit asking for rest breaks and concentrated on putting one foot down after the other. That got me through the day and the next one too.

One the third day out, Gabe promised, "Tomorrow we'll reach the lake where the biggest trout in the west are waiting for us. Very tasty. Hey, look here, by that fallen tree–mushrooms, nice big boletes. They're almost better than steak." Gabe picked several and laid them out on the ground. "We'll have these tomorrow along with our fish."

"Are you sure they're safe to eat?" I asked.

"You bet!" He turned one of the smaller mushrooms over. "Look at the bottom. Instead of having gills, it has tiny pores–like a sponge. That's an easy way to spot a bolete." Gabe broke it in half and handed me a piece. "Try it."

It tasted earthy and warm. I picked one for myself and chewed it with relish.

"There's more mushrooms over there." Gabe pointed to a promising patch a few yards above the trail. "I'm going after 'em."

We dropped our packs and climbed up the rocks. I saw the glint of metal up there at the same moment Gabe did–the jaws of a trap. The steel teeth gripped the paw of a large animal, spotted fur and white bone. The animal was gone, but a trail of dried blood led away from the trap.

Gabe frowned. "Barry, I don't like the looks of this. I'm going to follow the blood spots and see if I can find out what's happened."

The trail of blood led a few hundred feet along a rock ledge and into a stand of Ponderosa pines. We found the animal lying on its side, its teeth bared and its eyes glazed. It wasn't breathing. I saw the bloody stump where the right rear paw should have been.

"It's a lynx," Gabe said. "Damn those trappers!"

The cat had chewed off its paw trying to free itself from the trap, and then it had bled to death. There was nothing we could do for it.

As we resumed our hike, Gabe was unusually silent, and I knew he was thinking about the lynx we'd seen crossing the road. I wondered if it had occurred to him that nothing in the lynx's experience could have saved it from the trap.

Soon we began to hear the muffled roar of water rushing down the mountainside. It was almost half an hour before we reached its source, a river swollen with melt water thundering down its boulder-strewn bed.

Gabe said, "Once we cross this river, we'll come to a big meadow. Five miles beyond that is the lake where the trout are always biting."

I stared at the tumult. "This looks dangerous to me."

"Well, the river's higher and wilder than I've ever seen it," Gabe conceded. "The thaw came late this year, and lots of water is spilling off the peaks.

But we're strong, and this is really the best place to ford. It'll be okay."

Gabe moved into the stream, stepping from boulder to boulder, treading carefully on their slick surfaces. He was three-quarters of the way across when a rock shifted under him. He lost his balance and fell into the foaming water. The violent current tumbled him headfirst into the surge. The force of the water pinned his body against a huge boulder, while his hiking poles sailed downstream, bouncing from stone to stone.

The river terrified me, but I couldn't let Gabe die there. I grabbed my own hiking poles and followed Gabe's route across the boulders until I reached him. By then he'd quit struggling, and I was afraid he might already be dead. I dropped my own pack on the solid boulder I'd found and reached for him. Somehow I got hold of one of his pack straps, and I pulled on it with all the strength desperation could give me.

I lifted Gabe's head and shoulders out of the icy waves, but his right leg was caught on something under water. To reach his leg, I had to get his the pack off his body. I fought with the straps. They were waterlogged and wedged into their buckles. All the while the current dragged at him, and once I almost lost him. Finally I got the straps unfastened and shoved the pack away from him. It fell back into the water. I couldn't worry about it–I had to get Gabe free. I lay on my belly and manipulated his leg until I worked it loose. Only then could I drag him out of the river and onto the top of the boulder.

And there we were, one man standing and one man unconscious, caught in the middle of a wild and malevolent river with no help for God knew how many miles.

I looked at the spot on the river bank where the trail emerged. It wasn't as distant as I'd feared. I picked up my pack and heaved it toward the shore with both hands. It landed on solid ground just past the rushing water. My hiking poles went next.

Thank God Gabe weighed less than the stacks of iron plates I lifted at the gym. I manhandled him into a fireman's carry and stepped off onto the next likely boulder, avoiding the one that had betrayed Gabe. It was a long stretch to the next rock, but I made it. Then I ran out of rocks. I was going to have to wade the rest of the way–ten feet or so, I guessed. I stepped down into the torrent. The surge rocked me, but I braced myself and my legs held.

Every step came hard. The water came halfway up my thighs. Once I stepped into a hole and almost lost my balance, but I caught myself and plunged ahead to secure footing. Another six feet of fighting the current and I reached the bank. I lowered Gabe to the ground and rolled him onto his side. Water ran from his mouth, and he coughed. More water, more coughing. He opened his eyes and tried to say something. It came out as a wheeze.

"Quiet," I said. "And lie still."

But Gabe struggled to get up–and then he screamed, a long, ragged, hoarse cry. "My leg!"

"Easy, Gabe, easy," I said. "You're safe now."

"Barry?"

"I'm here. C'mon, I need to get those soaked clothes off you and get you warmed up."

"My leg . . . !"

I helped Gabe sit up so I could unlace his boots and have a look at the injury. The left boot came off easily. The right one was another matter. I tried to be gentle, but even so Gabe screamed again when I pulled off the right boot. His foot flopped awkwardly, and I guessed that his ankle was broken.

I got my sleeping bag out of my pack. Fortunately, it was still dry. I slipped Gabe's windbreaker off and peeled his sodden trousers away. After that I wrapped him in the sleeping bag.

"Good thing the tent was in my pack," I said. "I'll set it up as soon as I get a fire going. You need to eat something hot before hypothermia sets in. Come to think of it, so do I."

Our camp stove had been in Gabe's pack, which was probably halfway to Twin Spears by now. But the river had deposited plenty of branches and broken trees along this side of its banks, and some of it was dry enough to burn. Soon I had some chicken noodle soup cooking. By then Gabe was shivering so much I had to spoon-feed him.

Gabe's ankle had to be splinted. I found some small, slender branches and shaved them to size with my Swiss Army knife. Gabe had laughed when I bought that knife. "You need a buck knife like mine, not that greenhorn thing with a bunch of useless attachments," he'd said. But the knife he'd scorned did the job just fine.

When I began to manipulate his ankle, Gabe fainted. For that, I was grateful. I straightened the broken bones as best I could and splinted the leg with the whittled sticks and a couple of elastic bandages I'd brought along just in case I sprained something.

I'd gotten good with the tent and had it set up in no time. With my help, Gabe managed to push himself through the tent's door. Once he was inside, I rewrapped the sleeping bag around him and placed a log under his broken leg to elevate it.

Gabe began to talk. I could tell from the way he forced his words between his teeth that he was really hurting. "Barry, I'm sorry for this. I don't know how we're going to get out of this mess. Maybe you should go back to the trailhead and get help. I should be able to hold out here."

"No," I told him. "You can't walk. You can't keep a fire going or cook your own food. You'd never last as long as it would take me to get there. Besides, I'm not going to try crossing that river again. I'm staying with you until help arrives."

"How's that going to happen?" Gabe mumbled. "Nobody knows where we are."

"You let me figure that out," I said. I had no clue what to do next, but Gabe didn't need to know that.

"God, my leg hurts," he said. "I think I under-stand how that trapped lynx felt before it died."

"The lynx was alone. You're not, and I'm not going to let you die." My mind was beginning to make some sense out of our situation. "Here's what we'll do. I'll build a big smudge fire – God knows there's plenty of wet wood available. Then I'll make an SOS out of stones in that big open meadow out there. Maybe a plane will fly over. Someone is bound to spot us."

I hunted around in my pack for some aspirin and made Gabe swallow two of them along with some water from my Lexan bottle. His prized can-teen had been strapped to his pack and was long gone. "These'll help some with the pain," I said. I stripped off my own wet clothes and pulled on the reserve set from my pack. "I'm heading out to get the lay of the land. I'll be back soon."

On a hunch, I headed downriver, clambering over fallen trees and huge rocks, keeping as close to the water as I could. The river had been shoving whole trees onto this bank. Maybe it washed Gabe's pack up too.

I got lucky. After about an hour of scrambling alongside the water, I came to a log jam. There was Gabe's pack, snagged on a big pine branch far out in the stream and bobbing in the turbulence. The jam didn't look very stable. I didn't see how I was going to reach the pack, but I had to try. Our cell phone was in it, and so was most of the food we'd brought along.

I studied the tangle of broken timber. The jam had accumulated around an enormous pine log, and I climbed onto it, lying on my belly and wrapping my arms and legs around it as if I were shinnying up a tree. I inched along the log until I was close enough to the pack to snag it. When I pulled it loose, the whole mass of jumbled timbers shivered and threatened to break up. I held my breath until the pile stabilized. Then I began crawling back toward the shore, pulling the pack behind me.

I'd just slid off my log onto dry land when the jam came apart. My heart pounding, I watched as the river swept the timber away. But I was safe, and I had Gabe's pack. I checked out the contents. The sleeping bag, strapped to the top, was soaked and would be useless until it dried out, but the clothing inside was dry. The camp stove was still usable. The food packets were intact. But our cell phone had been smashed, and Gabe's old-fashioned canteen was missing.

Back at our makeshift camp, I found Gabe awake. "Good news," I told him. "I've got your pack–with the food."

"What about the cell phone?" he asked right away.

"Broken. But your flask of single-malt Scotch survived, and it's full."

Gabe tried to smile. "I could use a shot along about now."

I took it from the pack and let him take a swig. I awarded myself a swallow too. It warmed my throat and my belly, relieving the chill in my bones.

In the last light of the day, I got the smudge fire going and stoked up the campfire I'd built earlier until it was burning nice and hot. After that I hastily assembled a tripod of fallen branches and draped our soaked garments and Gabe's sleeping bag over it to dry. I'd have to get through the coldest hours of the night with only a single extra layer of clothes and whatever heat the fire reflected toward our tent.

We didn't sleep well. Every time Gabe dozed off, the pain woke him, and I got up often to put more wood on both our fires. At first light, I boiled water for making coffee and freeze-dried eggs for our breakfast. After I'd given Gabe a couple more aspirin, he felt strong enough to sit up and eat by himself.

It took a long time to assemble enough big rocks to make a visible SOS in the meadow, but finally I was satisfied with my work. After that, all I could do was wait and hope. Once I thought I heard a plane overhead and rushed out to see, but there was nothing in the sky except buzzards spiraling on the thermals. I hoped the birds weren't considering us for their dinner.

I kept busy maintaining the smudge fire, but there wasn't much I could do to help Gabe except feed him and dose him with aspirin. We passed the hours by discussing legal cases, and when we couldn't stand that any longer, by inventing murder mysteries. Some of them were pretty good, and I hoped we'd live long enough to publish them.

Two full days went by. Our supply of aspirin and Scotch was getting low, and Gabe was developing a fever.

On the fourth day, Gabe couldn't talk sense. His forehead was sizzling hot, and he was rambling in delirium. I heard him repeat, "Amy, Amy, Amy," over and over again. Sometimes he called out for his mother, sometimes for his father. Sometimes he just babbled about fishing, about points of law, about pizza–good Lord, we both could have used a pizza then–about the lynx and the trap and about chains binding him.

I'd never been a religious man, but during the next 24 hours I prayed nonstop to every deity I could think of. I had exhausted all the burnable wood near our campsite and was headed downstream to find a new supply when I heard hoofbeats and voices. I started yelling, "Help! Up here! Oh, God, help!"

If they hadn't been wearing Stetsons, I might have mistaken the oncoming riders for angels, but then I recognized them–the hands from Twin Spears. Steve Mitchell, the wrangler who'd warned us about the dangers of our hiking expedition, was leading the pack.

"You boys have a problem?" he asked when he reached me.

"You bet we do! My friend broke his ankle fording the river, and he's got a bad fever now. Our cell phone's broken, and I didn't know how I was going to get him some help."

"Somebody up there must be looking out for you," Steve said. "This morning I found your pal's old canteen floating in a pond where the river flows into the flats by the ranch. Then one of the guys noticed the smoke from your smudge fire. Son, that fire was a damn good idea. Between it and the canteen, we figured you must have gotten into real trouble, so we saddled up and came looking."

Steve carried a working cell phone, and he called for a medevac helicopter. Soon Gabe was the center of attention at the hospital in Sheridan. Within 24 hours, Gabe's father, his mother and sisters arrived, along with Gabe's faithful light of love, the auburn-haired, dark-eyed Amy. They all insisted on staying until the doctors agreed that Gabe was out of danger.

From then on, everything ran smoothly. The docs pinned Gabe's ankle back together and outfitted him with a walking cast. Gabe's family headed home for Colorado.

Amy and I took Gabe back to Chicago. I drove Gabe's big Expedition and Amy rode shotgun. Gabe was stretched out on the back seat, ensconced in heaps of pillows. He wasn't saying much about the glorious freedoms of the wilderness anymore, but maybe that was because he was loaded full of painkillers.

I had to give Gabe credit for guts and determination. A week after we got home, he returned to work. On that Monday morning, he asked me to come into his office and close the door.

"What's up?" I asked. "Tough case? Need some help?"

"I have a confession to make," Gabe said.

"I'm not a priest," I protested.

"No, but you're the guy I owe. I thought I was better than you. I was the wilderness expert and you were the greenhorn. I was the free soul, the wild cat. You were the domesticated guy who couldn't live without other people."

"It's okay. Forget about it. I have."

"I'm not done. That lynx . . . . Something my dad said to me at the hospital: 'Son, you're nothing like a lynx. You're a link–a link in a chain of people you love and people who love you.' When I was in the hospital, I spent a lot of time thinking about that. My pride nearly killed both you and me. You're one of the strongest links in my chain, Barry. You saved my life. It shames me to admit this, but you're a better man than I am."

What the hell was I supposed to say to that? "Gabe, you'd have done the same for me," I finally replied, and I never doubted it.

"And then there's Amy," Gabe added. "What was the matter with me, that I couldn't understand how much she loves me–and how much I love her? Well, I understand now. By the way, I want you to be the best man at our wedding."

"You and Amy–?"

"I humbled myself and proposed to her." Gabe smiled. "She actually said yes. We're planning a big wedding for next year, in August."

If Gabe could swallow some pride, I guess I could too. "You know, Gabe, when I look back at our adventure, I realize it made a better man out of me too. I discovered that I could be strong and resourceful when I needed to be. But I never did get to catch a trout. Do you think we could go up into the mountains again before your wedding? I'd like you to show me how to snag the big ones."

"Absolutely." Gabe stretched out his hand, and we shook on it.

Cold Vengeance

If you lived on the north side of the city, you often saw them—wheeled pushcarts laden with fruit-flavored ice cream bars—mango, papaya, and coconut. Steered by old Mexican men with proud mustaches, the carts announced their coming with a rack of bells that chimed at every bump in the asphalt. It was a happy summer sound.

On the sultriest days the ice cream vendors did well. Gringos and Latinos alike crowded around the carts, choosing their favorite flavors, stripping the sticky paper wrapping from the bars and letting the sweet ices soothe their heat-parched throats.

Then came the day that one such *abuelo* steered his mobile ice cream parlor straight toward the two street punks. It never occurred to the old grandfather to be afraid until the first fist smashed into his face. More punches followed, and then a kick to the gut that knocked him backwards onto the hot pavement. The punks seized the grimy dollar bills and quarters and dimes he'd spent the whole day earning. With the *abuelo's* money tucked into their pockets, they overturned the cart, spilling all the ice cream bars onto the asphalt.

It happened so fast that no one could help. The punks hot-footed it into the alleys and soon vanished. The old man struggled to his feet and carefully picked up his melting inventory, stacking the ruined ice cream bars neatly into the insulated compartment of his cart. Then he sat down on the curb, blood dripping from his broken nose, almost but not quite crying. He may have been an old *señor* past his prime, but he still had his pride, and he would not give in to weeping.

Someone with a cell phone offered to call the police.

"Please no call," the old man mumbled through swollen lips.

A well-dressed woman whispered to the would-be caller, "He probably doesn't have a green card."

Sometimes even old immigrant men have their guardians. Someone did make a phone call, but not to the cops. Soon the *abuelo's* eldest son came and took his father and the pushcart home in his rusty truck. Then the sons of his sons, staunch members of the Latin Kings, put the word out on the streets.

Revenge, when it came, was sweet. It took months. The perpetrators had gone into hiding. But there was good business to be done in the neighbor-hood, plenty of drugs to buy and sell, and so one snowy winter day they returned to their old haunts. The punks had their fellow gangbangers to back them up, but they failed to reckon with their deter-mined Latino counterparts.

Soon the Latin lads exacted their justice. Spying the punks emerging from a liquor store, they sur-rounded the pair and hustled them at gunpoint into the back seat of an ancient Ford sedan. They held the punks at the muzzles of their guns and forced them into a garage in a seldom-used alley. In the center of the structure stood the old vendor's pushcart, filled to capacity with cold, sweet desserts — ice cream bars flavored with mango, papaya and coconut.

The Mexican boys bound the terrified gang-bangers to scarred wooden chairs and force-fed them the entire contents of the cart, until both of the punks had ice cream dripping from their chins onto their baggy shirts and their hip-hop pants. Hot tears blistered their cheeks as ice cream streamed down their necks and chests. Their eyes scrunched tight as ice cream headaches clenched cold fingers around their brains, and they moaned wetly as their super-cooled stomachs rebelled and ejected the icy treats. Liquefied ice cream pooled all over the greasy con-crete floor.

Nor was that the worst of it. The Latino boys pummeled the sick and shivering thieves with fists and feet, just as the gangbangers had done to the old grandfather. They finished by dragging the stunned pair into the deep snowdrifts in the alley.

Acting on an anonymous tip, the police found the bedraggled punks where they lay in the snow.

"We ought to leave these scumbags here until they freeze their balls off," the rotund Irish patrolman muttered in disgust. "They'll never be any use to society."

His partner, a sturdy black woman, cuffed the smaller punk, grabbed hold of his arms and dragged him to the squad car. "C'mon, Paddy, we still have to do our duty. Let's get these assholes down to the county hospital."

At the emergency room door, orderlies strapped each one of the pair onto a gurney, handling them as roughly as inanimate objects. "Does anyone really care about these two?" one ER doc inquired.

The Irish cop barked out a harsh laugh. "Hell, no. They're just a couple of gangbangers who pushed the Mexicans a little too hard and got what they deserved. Do what you want with 'em. We'll come and haul 'em off to jail in the morning."

The emergency room docs studied the new arrivals and concluded they didn't care either. Too many good people who really deserved medical care were waiting their turn. So they let the punks cool their frost-bitten heels on the gurneys through the night, applied a few bandages in the morning, and turned them over to the police.

When the crestfallen pair got their day in court, the judge sentenced them to spend their nights in the jail and their days pushing ice cream carts in the neighborhood just outside it—one of the roughest neighborhoods in the city. They sold mango, papaya, and coconut ice cream bars to scores of eager children. Their former pals sometimes came around to laugh at them and to steal their meager earnings.

It was still better than enduring the cold vengeance of the Latino vigilantes.

birds & beasts

Follow your bliss.

—Joseph Campbell

The Bebop Bugaroos

"Don't try to fool me with that silly old fairy tale," snapped Proud Millicent. "I'm a fine, educated lady, not some stupid peasant girl from the village indulging in wishful thinking." She quite managed to discount the fact that the large knobby toad sitting on the rock in her path was addressing her in words her human ears understood perfectly well. Brushing a lock of her glossy golden hair out of her lustrous blue eyes, she snarled at the creature, "I would never, never kiss the likes of something as slimy and ugly as you. Hop away and get out of my sight!"

Plink! A musical chime sounded in Millicent's ear. She looked around for the source of the sound.

To her surprise, she saw nothing that seemed familiar. The path through the trees had vanished. A jagged cliff loomed high where she thought the rock had been. Thick green stems surrounded her like a forest of saplings. Looking up, she saw green leaves large as umbrellas and purple blossoms big as dinner plates. Violets? Yes, violets. But so big!

A large, black, shiny object came down upon the flowers, crushing them. A reflection appeared on its polished surface: a creepy-crawly segmented worm with a pair of legs attached to every segment. Its minute black eyes peered back at her. Oh, no, it could not be — but it had to be — her own reflection.

Before Millicent could shriek, she heard a thunderous "ahem!" from on high. She stretched herself as tall as she could until she could see past the enormous shoe — for that was what had crushed the violets — to a dirty lavender dress embellished with torn ecru lace. The garment seemed to extend to the heavens. At last she focused on a pair of dull brown eyes in a doughy face surrounded by tangles of black hair. A giantess! An ogress?

"No, my dear, I am neither a giantess nor an ogress," boomed the female whatever-it-was. "It's merely that you have shrunk. You are Proud Millicent no longer. From this day forth, you are Millypede, doomed to run forever from my little pet, Bufo the Toad, here on his rock. For, you see, those peasant girls you believe are stupid are actually correct. Witches exist, and to offend a witch is to invite being transformed into something as unlovely as your temperament. I am a witch, and my name is — but no, I shall not tell you my name. If you knew it, you could free yourself and become Millicent again—perhaps."

The witch continued, "Now, Bufo the Toad once was Bruno the Bold, son of King Wilibert the Wise. Bruno was handsome of face but as cold-hearted as any amphibian. I begged him for a kiss, as he begged you, and like you he could not see past an ugly surface. He spurned me. So he became as you see him now. You, my dear Milly-pede, are quite as arrogant as Bufo, so I thought it proper to transform you into a creature as nasty as your pride. And so you both shall remain, Bufo doomed to pursue you, and you condemned to run from him, for if he catches you, he will swallow you down." And with that, the witch turned and walked away, her footsteps shaking the earth.

Bufo hopped down from his rock, flicking his tongue, looking for his promised meal. Milly tried to dodge, but she hadn't yet learned to synchronize her abundance of legs. Terrified, she rolled herself into a tight ball, expecting to become Bufo's breakfast in the next instant.

The toad popped Milly into his gaping maw, only to spit her out again. "Faugh!" he cried, and tried to wash out the taste of her with gulps of dew from the flowers. "You taste terrible! The witch lied to us! I can't possibly eat you. Milly cautiously unrolled her body, a segment at a time, and tried her legs again. They began to move as a millipede's should. She could have scuttled away, but she realized she had nothing to fear from Bufo.

A shadow passed overhead. A bird. Insect instinct told Millie that a bird was truly something to fear.

"Dear Bufo," she pleaded, "forgive me my cruelty and protect me, for I am a weak little thing, and you are a big, strong creature."

"Why should I help you, you stuck-up, mean little bug?" replied Bufo. "Why, you are no use to anyone. You're not even good to eat. And you are certainly uglier than any toad."

"I'm afraid," Milly whimpered. "I want my Mama."

"Well, your Mama certainly won't help you now," Bufo said. "In fact, if she saw you, she'd probably scream and squash you with her delicate little slipper. Too bad for you."

"What about you? You can't exactly ride a fine horse home to a royal welcome in your father's household, either. I can just imagine how the butler would deal with a hoptoad in the hall."

Bufo gave her a squint-eyed stare, no easy matter for a toad. "I'm hungry. I need to find something to eat."

"Well, since I can't be your dinner, let me come with you. At least you're somebody I can talk to."

"I guess that would be all right," Bufo said. "But you'll have to run fast, for I can hop at great speed." As if to prove it, he began bounding away.

"Wait, wait!" shrieked Milly. "I may have lots of legs, but they're all short. I can't keep up!"

"How sad," said Bufo. "Good-bye, then."

But he hesitated, and Milly, who after all had been an intelligent young lady, said, "Leave me, then, if you want to be a toad forever. But it seems to me that if we stay together, maybe we can find a way to become human again."

Bufo saw her point. "I guess I could carry you. Climb up on my back and hang on—here we go!"

And so they began their wandering. Bufo dined on unwary flies, and Milly burrowed into the earth to swallow the littlest of subterranean bugs. It was a life, after a fashion. Thus they existed until one day they encountered a large black cricket. Bufo began edging closer. The cricket would fill his tummy for quite a long time. But the insect saw its peril. It stood up on four of its six legs and began to chirp a lively tune. It sounded like a tiny trumpet. Bufo found the music irresistible, for after all, he had not always been a toad. When he had been a prince, he had loved to sing and dance. He began to sing along in the rough fashion of toads, producing a drumlike accompaniment to the cricket's brassy squawks.

Wow, maybe we have something here, thought Milly. She knew how to play the piano in her parents' drawing room, but there was no piano here in the woods. Even if there were, she was now too tiny to play a note. Still, she had a good sense of rhythm, the result of managing her multitudinous legs. She raised herself up upon her rearmost segments and waggled back and forth as though conducting an orchestra.

When the tune was over and before Bufo recollected his intent to eat the cricket, the new acquaintance began to speak. "I am called Gryllo," he said, "and I wasn't always like this."

"Of course you weren't," muttered Milly. "An ugly witch—"

"I was once a renowned musician named Jasper the Jazzy," continued the cricket. "But a mean old witch came to me and insisted that I play for her alone. My music is too good to waste on the likes of her, and I refused. So she turned me into a bug."

Bufo and Milly nodded in sympathy. Bufo flicked out an agile tongue and snagged a passing gnat. Although he was still quite hungry, he decided he could delay the further gratification of his appetite, sparing Gryllo for the sake of the music.

"Gryllo, Milly, and I are looking for the way to become human again," the toad explained. "You may come with us, if you would like. At least we could enjoy a tune now and then."

And so the three set off, wandering through meadow and wood, always asking other small creatures if they knew the name of the witch. But for a long time, they discovered none that were able to talk. Even if those wee animals and insects knew something helpful, they had no way to speak of it.

Then one sunny afternoon, as Gryllo chirped out "Toad went a'courtin," and Bufo boomed along, a pudgy green katydid fluttered to rest on a nearby coneflower stalk. "Katydid-katydidn't," she trilled by way of introduction. Waving her transparent green-veined wings, she joined in the song, singing "Toadie went a courtin' and he did ride." Feeling creative, Bufo harmonized, "Mmm-hmm, mmm-hmm."

When the song ended, Milly asked, "Katy, what did you or didn't you do to end up like this?"

"It's what I didn't do," sniffed the bug. "A big ugly witch —"

"We know," sighed Bufo. "She asked you to sing for her. And Katy didn't, did you, Katy?"

"Of course I didn't," replied the katydid. "I was once Catherine the Coloratura, famed throughout the known world. I had a voice that could soar—crowds of people came to hear my performances. Why would I sing for a filthy witch who wouldn't even ante up the price of admission to my concerts? I called my serving man to have her removed from my presence. But before he arrived, the witch turned me into this—insect. My serving man tried to swat me dead. Luckily my dressing room window was open, and I flew out before his blow landed."

"Care to join our band?" Gryllo asked hopefully.

"What, come along with you ugly bugs? Is there any money in it?"

Bufo tried to laugh, but his toad throat wasn't designed for it.

"No money," pronounced Milly. "As you noticed, we're just bugs, after all. Even you. Especially you. We are journeying together in the hope of discovering a way to become human again."

Katy shook out her wings. "Well, now that you put it that way, I guess I'll come along. This life doesn't offer many opportunities even for a famous diva like me."

Off they marched, performing when the weather was good, and frogs and toads, mayflies and dragonflies and all manner of wee creatures gathered to listen. This worked especially well for Bufo, who often dined on members of the audience—after the concert was over, of course.

One sunny afternoon the little band of bugs came upon a nest of carpenter ants busily reshaping a fallen tree branch into sawdust and shavings. "Why do you just destroy the wood?" asked curious Milly. "Couldn't you make something useful out of it?" She didn't really expect an answer, since only animals that had once been people could talk.

"Such as?" demanded the big boss ant.

"So who were you when you were human?" asked Bufo. He would have liked to eat the boss ant, but he had learned the hard way not to snare bugs that could bite or sting his tender tongue.

"Alvar the Architect I am. An evil day it was when a nasty old witch asked me to design her new kitchen cabinets—"

"We know all about it," chorused the members of the bug band.

"The job was not worthy of my great talent, so I turned it down. And then the witch transformed me and my crew into ants."

"You didn't answer my question," complained Milly. "Why don't you build something?"

"Such as?"

"For instance . . . could you build me a piano?"

Alvar sneered. "What for, you insignificant little creepy-crawly? You don't have fingers for playing it."

"But I have legs—lots of them. More than enough to reach all 88 keys. Please?"

"Yes, a piano—that's exactly the instrument we need," Gryllo chimed in.

Katy sighed wistfully. "I do miss my piano accompanist. Every singer needs one."

Convinced, Alvar and his crew set to work. After all, they had nothing better to do. While they sawed and hammered, Bufo and the bug band played lively songs to keep the ants energized. Finally a tiny piano emerged.

"Oh, it's lovely!" Milly stretched her segmented body along the length of the keyboard. Tentatively she played a few notes. Soon something resembling a waltz emerged. And then, to the delight of her companions and all of the ants, she launched into buggy-woogie.

"We're the Bebop Bugaroos!" crowed Bufo. Gryllo trumpeted along and Katy began scatting a rhythmic riff. Alvar and his crew danced wildly around the band.

The earth began to shake.

The Bugaroos stopped playing, all but Milly.

"It's the witch!" cried Bufo in alarm. "Hide, all of you, or she'll stomp us!"

But Milly was oblivious. As the others fled to shelter, her tiny feet danced joyfully on the keys. She couldn't remember having been so happy, not even as a human.

"Milly, get away!" groaned Bufo. "She'll kill you!" He looked up just in time to see the hem of the witch's filthy lavender dress skim the tops of the wild asters. He had to act. Hopping bravely out of hiding, he pulled Milly from the piano and tossed her onto his back. But before he could escape with her, the witch had picked him up. He found himself and Milly cupped in the witch's greasy palm. One squeeze, and they'd both be dead.

"Before we die, Bufo, I'd like you to know something," whispered Milly. "I love you. You have been my savior and my friend. Farewell."

"My little thousand-legged darling," Bufo whispered in reply, "Surely we'll meet on the other side —

"Don't be silly," boomed the witch. "I think you've all learned your lesson–that ugly is as ugly does and beauty is where you find it. Now I'd like to offer you Bebop Bugaroos a deal. If you and your hidden friends promise to play your music for me whenever I ask, I'll restore you to your proper forms. Of course, you know what will happen if you refuse!"

"So we don't really need to know your true name?" Milly bravely inquired.

"Don't push your luck," said the witch. "Today you do not need my true name, for your music has made me feel mellow. Now, will you all accept the deal I am offering?"

"We accept," chorused the toad, the millipede, the cricket and the katydid.

"What about us?" cried all the carpenter ants.

"My castle is in dire need of renovation. Remodel it for me, and all will be forgiven," said the witch. "Make sure you don't forget the kitchen cabinets!"

She put Bufo and Milly on the ground and snapped her fingers. A flash like a lightning bolt crashed to earth, and when the light died, a little group of people stood staring at each other — Bruno the Bold, handsome in princely riding attire, Proud Millicent, now properly humbled but nonetheless clad in elegant finery, Jasper the Jazzy in real cool hipcat duds, Catherine the Coluratura encased in a skin-tight satin gown that showed off her feminine curves, Alvar the Architect in a Hong-Kong tailored business suit, and his work crew ready to work in their overalls. In front of them all stood the witch, now clad in a flashy outfit by Prada, her black clod-hoppers replaced by Jimmy Choo stilettos, and her snowy white hair falling in soft waves to her shoulders—as lovely a woman as you'd ever hope to see.

Alvar the Architect restored the witch's castle and his renown spread until he became the premier castle designer for all the realm. He and all his crew became rich.

Jasper the Jazzy met his match in Catherine the diva, and soon they were wed. Prince Bruno married Proud Millicent and made her his princess. Soon there were children, and then many children.

Like all married folk, sometimes the young couples needed a night away from the nursery, and so they turned to the most trustworthy babysitter they could find: the witch. She loved children, and she amused the little ones while their parents went out on the town.

It was the children who finally learned her true name: Grandma.

And for all their long lives, the Bebop Bugaroos played their merry music for Grandma whenever she asked.

Bird in Flight

The bronze-green parrot peered in all directions, craning his neck and bobbing his head to see around the obstruction of the man's hat. The dark eyes fell upon leafless trees, ridge after ridge of Tennessee forest that had not yet awakened from winter's sleep. Inside him ancestral memories stirred, recalling a place his species knew but where he had never been. Mountains like these, he thought, except the trees on those mountains would be lush and green, watered by daily rains rising from a warm shallow sea and breathing out the scents of ripe fruits.

But these mountains might do.

The bird, who had passed season after season isolated among people, away from his own kind, possessed a capacity for thought and imagination that might have frightened his giant companions, had they suspected it. If he could talk, he might have told them, but his species had only a small capacity for imitating human speech.

He longed to fly. In all his years, he had never flown. The first human he had known, another man, had pulled the flight feathers from one wing. The man had carried him in his cage to places where many birds congregated but were never allowed to flock. Like him, they huddled alone in wire cages. Now and then someone would come, take up a bird and study it. It had happened to him. Human hands stretched out his undamaged wing, remarking on the beauty of its blue and green feathers. Human eyes studied his markings: the cap of white feathers on his head, the iridescent bronze of his shoulders, the surprise of bright red feathers under his tail. Human hands gave the man who had brought him a soft-looking piece of cloth, two strips of yellow ribbon descending from a flowerlike yellow rosette.

"Is that the best you can do?" the man asked. "Only a third place?"

"You should be pleased. The competition was stiff. Maybe in another show, he would do better," answered a woman in white. The man seemed disappointed and took the bird away to a new place. He never again saw that man and did not care, even though that was the only companion the bird had ever known. The man, after all, had not cared for him.

For nearly three seasons after that, he endured in a cage within a stack of cages, each one confining a bird of some kind. Sometimes a bird was taken from its wire prison, never to return. In this place other kinds of animals waited their destinies. These creatures were variously called, he learned as he listened—for there was little else to do—dogs, cats, hamsters, guinea pigs, chinchillas. They had cages of their own. Eventually, they too would depart, and others took their places.

During this time, the missing flight feathers on his wing tried to grow back. But the quills in their thick horny sheaths hurt as they emerged. He didn't need the feathers, for there was no room for him to fly. So, to stop the pain, he chewed them off.

On a cold day—he could tell by the blasts of frigid air that entered this place when a door opened, which it seemed to do constantly—a man and a woman took a particular interest in him. The man picked him up and smoothed his feathers. The parrot felt an attraction. He uttered a small croak of contentment—for he did not have a pretty voice, unlike the canaries and the finches—and butted his head insistently at the man's arm. He heard a sound that he had learned to recognize as a human's way of displaying pleasure, a soft chuckling noise. And then hands placed him, quite carefully and gently, into a small square space enclosed by clear walls–a cage of a sort, he realized. Holes in the walls let in air, and the bottom of the space had been cushioned by some kind of material that felt soft and good under his toes.

All went dark when the woman carefully placed another piece of cloth atop the cage. The cage felt like a hollow carved into an old tree. His kind nested in such places. The cage was lifted and carried out into the cold for a moment. Then he heard noise and sensed vibration. This, he remembered, came from some kind of conveyance. People could not fly, he understood, but they could travel by placing themselves in enclosed spaces that ate up distance at speeds almost as fast as a determined parrot might fly.

He was not surprised to find another cage awaiting him when the cloth was removed from the plastic carrier. The man he had instinctively liked, together with the woman who was the man's mate, had prepared a home for him, bigger than the one he had left behind. He saw dishes filled with water and food, and perches upon which he could climb or sleep. He sipped at the water. The food could wait; he wasn't hungry. Inside one corner of the cage, shielding the bare wires, dangled a cluster of rainbow feathers. The cluster resembled a bird, and it comforted him. He snuggled up to it. When he did, the humans made noises of pleasure.

Whenever they approached his cage, they repeated short bursts of sound, the same noises each time. Parry, Parry, they said to him, and told him it was short for parrot. In time, he recognized it. He understood that it was to be his name, at least among humans. If his kind had names of their own, he did not know what his might be. He learned to imitate the human voices: Pretty Parry. Good Parry. Pretty Bird. He learned the human's names too, but he could not compel his throat to make the sounds.

With this man and woman, he lived for many seasons, far beyond his ability to count. Sometimes he had companions. The first was a noisy gray bird who didn't stay long. Then came two colorful little birds of a kind he had known from the place of many birds and animals. Parakeets. He could almost say that sound. He liked them, for they sang to him and preened the feathers on his head. But they were short-lived little things. First one fell sick and then the other. When they died, he understood loss.

His humans allowed him to leave his cage for hours at a time. He perched on top and watched their lives. Sometimes the feathers on his damaged wing grew out, and he tried to fly. The man encouraged him, holding him so that he could flap. He developed flight muscles. But the new feathers came in weak, and always he ended by chewing them off. His every attempt at flight ended with a beak-first fall to the ground.

His humans sometimes took him outside, to the woods, where he perched upon the man's shoulder as they walked among the trees. He found joy in these excursions, glorying in the wind, the wild green, the songs of the free birds and even the open blue sky, although when a shadow passed overhead, he took cover under his man's hat brim. Shadows high above, his instinctual memory, meant hawks, and hawks sought birds like him as prey.

In time, his humans left their home, the nest he had shared with them for so long, and put themselves into a smaller one. They took him along. In many ways their new nest resembled the one they had left, with places where they could perch and where they could eat and where they could sleep.

But it could move. As it moved into unfamiliar regions, he saw new kinds of land and heard new kinds of birds and smelled new smells.

They left their old nest in the season of young leaves and moved from place to new place through the season of ripe apples and corn and into what should have been the season of falling leaves and then into the season of falling snow. But the leaves did not fall, nor did the snow. He had intelligence enough to understand that his humans had gradually migrated south, far south from where he had lived with them for so many seasons.

Soon they moved again, into a bigger nest that stood firmly upon the ground. They placed his wire cage on a table out in a large, open space, where he could see much farther than he was accustomed to. He liked that, liked to watch his humans and others who came to visit. Often, for the weather was almost always warm, the humans opened doors and windows, and he could hear birds, all kinds, singing, clucking and chattering in the trees beyond. Sometimes he heard the shrill kee-ah, kee-ah, kee-ah of the hawks. Even though he knew the hawks could not reach him in the human nest, he cowered in the back of his cage when they called to each other.

Once again the man let the parrot perch upon his shoulder and walked with him through a forest. This forest was unlike any the bird had yet seen. He sensed something familiar in the moist woods, where frogs pip-pipped and huge ungainly reptiles slithered into a river as the man's steps crackled upon dead leaves and twigs.

His flight feathers grew again. He ceased chewing them off. As usual, the man encouraged him to attempt flight. Little by little he gained strength. On the woodland walks, he succeeded in flying a little farther each day. But he soon tired, dropped to the ground and waited, panting, for the familiar hand to lift him up. Always restless, the humans one day set him into the clear-walled cage in which they carried him on their journeys. He was used to it. He tasted spring in the air, and he wanted to stay in the new nest, but he had no choice. He went where they went.

They went north. He felt the air change slowly, becoming more chill. The fresh green scent of growing things diminished, and the sun grew more pale. If he could have spoken, he would have told them, "Wrong! I am a bird of the south. Wrong to take me away!" But he could not, and the journey continued.

At last they stopped in a place where the rising spring had not yet arrived. The man took him into a forest that he recognized. He and his human had walked here before, on that first trip south. He knew the name of this place: Tennessee. It sounded like birdsong. He had seen the mountains upon which these trees grew, and he had longed for the freedom they promised. But then he could not fly.

The man carried him up, higher and higher, until he could see the line of forested ridges. He opened his wings just a little away from his body and felt the cold breeze against his breast. But that was all right; his thick feathers insulated him well. His kind had been born to the chill air of high places.

He attempted flight, fluttered to the ground. Only a short flight, that had been. The man picked him up, and the parrot rested as the man walked.

The wind rose. The parrot stretched himself tall. Could he fly? If he did, could he find his way back to his companion?

He spread his wings and sprang up in the same moment, just as the man realized his intent. Too late. He caught the wind just as the man's hand brushed by him, and he flew at last. The open sky beckoned.

The man called out to him. "Parry! Parry! Come back!"

He turned his eye back to look, just for a moment. Let me fly, let me fly, he begged the wind. He soared on its currents, and below him flashed the bare-limbed trees, the gleam of stream-filled valleys, the sharp crests of the ridges. He rose above them all, flying for the first time in his life.

Then his muscles failed him. He managed to hold his wings outspread until he could break his fall in a tall tree, claws fastening onto a thick branch and holding him—just—as he tottered on the unfamiliar perch. He panted and wheezed. Off in the distance, he could hear the man, his companion, calling in a voice that grew increasingly hoarse, but he could neither reply nor return. After a while, he no longer heard the sound of his human name.

He perched in the tree for a very long time. The light faded from the cloudy sky, and night enveloped the mountains. He slept despite the wintry chill.

Dawn woke him as it did the birds of the forest. He added his harsh cries to their morning trills, their whistles, their caws. If he were still in his cage, he would have broken his fast with bits of egg, of bread, of the seed pellets his humans gave him. But they were not here, and he was hungry. He sampled a fat bud on the branch where he had perched. Bitter, but it would do.

He attempted flight. The muscles of his breast, stiffened from yesterday's exertions, ached when he tried his wings, but they obeyed him. He moved from branch to branch, dropping a little lower in the tree each time. Perhaps nearer the ground he might find seeds or fruit. Instinct told him what to look for. But winter still held sway, and what he sought was scarce.

He grew stronger as the days passed. Little by little he moved south, finding nourishment in the new leaves just opening. Now and then he sampled a crawling creature and found it tolerable eating.

But as he sought to eat, other creatures sought to eat him. One night a large furred creature with dark bands around its eyes almost caught him in the hollow tree where he rested, but he awakened to the sound of its coming and slipped out into the moonlight, fluttering higher and higher into the tree. The creature could not follow him into the fragile topmost branches. After that he sought hollows in higher places.

On the ground he met animals that reminded him of the dogs that humans kept as companions. A small reddish one pounced at him as he stripped the last of winter's shriveled berries from a low bush, but he flew up in time. A larger, browner animal much like the first, with a skimpy brush of a tail, eyed the parrot hungrily, but that one's clumsy leap fell well short of the now-wary bird. He heard its whine of frustration as he took to the air.

He understood cats. In that place full of animals where he had lived for a time, the cats watched the birds with avid eyes. He knew their insatiable hunger for his kind. He smelled cat in the mountains and saw one once, bigger than those he had known, with a short tail and a yellow coat spotted with black. He feared that beast more than any he had yet encountered. After that, any hint of cat smell sent him winging farther on.

Parrots by nature mass in flocks. Lonely, missing his human companions, the bird sought to find a way back to them, the only flock he knew. Where was the nest in which his man and his woman had installed him? He knew that it lay south. But how far? Or was he really looking for something else, a place where others of his kind soared together, borne on the sea wind?

As he flew, he hunted for others like himself. The mountain forests teemed with birds, solitary birds, nesting pairs and flocks migrating to their northern ranges. They neither welcomed nor rejected him. They simply displayed indifference.

He despaired of reaching any sanctuary. His flight was strong, it was true, but not as fast as it should have been. The feathers that had finally emerged on his damaged wing had never grown in perfectly, like those on the good wing. Whole sections of vanes were missing. Barbules refused to interlock as they should. Perhaps in his next molt, better ones would replace these. Until then, he had to manage with what existed.

He flew on. The air grew warmer, the mountains higher and greener. At so great a height, he should have seen fate coming, but soft clouds full of moisture obscured the sun, and the soaring peregrine cast no shadow. Only at the last moment did the parrot glimpse its nemesis. He did his best to dodge and swerve, but the damaged wing could not execute the swift maneuvers that might have extricated him from the falcon's outstretched talons. The abrupt jerk as the falcon halted the parrot's flight broke the smaller bird's neck.

Yet he flew on. He no longer flew alone. A cloud of bright green and yellow birds enveloped him in their brightness. "What are you," he called, and for the first time in his life a bird answered him.

"We are like you and not like you," the other bird said in a language of whistles and shrieks that the bronze parrot could understand. "We belong to this land. We are bound here. But you do not belong."

"I don't understand," the parrot cried, a vague memory of pain and shock nudging at his mind.

"You are dead. We are dead," said the bright green bird. "Once thousands of living birds like us fed and nested and played here. Thousands. People killed us, first a red people who wanted our feathers for their headdresses, and then a paler people who grudged us a tithe of their crops. Now our kind is gone, but our spirits remain bound to the land that once nurtured us."

"Then what am I?" the parrot begged to know.

"Our cousin. That is why we have come to you. You don't belong here. You must go."

"Where? Where?"

"Where were you going when the falcon killed you?"

"South. South to my humans. Where else?"

"We cannot tell you. But if you stay here, you will always be alone, and your spirit cannot find contentment."

The bright bird faded back into its flock, which wheeled and swerved away, fading into a high cloud in the distance.

The bronze parrot might have wept, had it been within his capability. Instead, he looked below, down to the mountains which had been raised not once but many times, worn down by wind and rain and elevated again by forces within the earth. If the mountains could survive so many attempts to destroy them, so could he. The falcon's strike, far from annihilating him, had transmuted him from living bird to pure spirit. He existed still, as changeless as only the dead can be.

He stretched his wings, gaining speed. He flew as he had never flown before, turning and dodging and darting, flight feathers catching the light, glistening in their blue-green perfection. Every feather showed smooth and complete, as it should be. He danced on the wind and caught a thermal, soaring. He did not know where he was going, but he would know when he found it.

As he flew by a place he could not name, the bird sensed a familiar presence. Close by, in the world of living things, the man who had loved him mourned his loss. He slowed his flight and circled nearby.

"I died," the bird told the man, "and I am going south."

With strong, powerful beats of his wings, he rose again to the welcoming sky. Somewhere ahead green mountains beside a blue-green sea awaited him.

He flew on.

fantastic worlds

'Twas in the merry month of May
When green buds all were swelling,
Sweet William to the dooryard came
A'courting Barb'ry Allen.

— Adapted from traditional folk song

Barb'ry Allen Tells All

By now, just about every soul in England has heard the ballad: "In Scarlet Town where I was born, there was a fair maid dwellin,' and every youth cried well-a-day, her name was Barb'ry Allen." The broadsides have been spreading faster than the French pox, passed from hand to hand and ear to ear until everyone with any pretensions to being a musician has been forced to learn the song and, what's more, sing it upon demand. And demanded it is.

As the story goes, a lad known as Sweet William courted Barb'ry Allen, who rejected his suit. Unlike any sensible man, who would have just gone off and found himself a more willing wench, William laid himself down and perished, for love, he told his mother. When he died, young Barb'ry repented of her hard-hearted treatment of the wretched William and — according to the song — decided that she would follow him to the grave. The ballad recounts how they were buried side by side, and out of each grave, we are told, there grew a plant that suggested their respective natures: from his emerged a red rose and from hers a thorny briar. Please! Let no one remark that the rose, no matter how lovely, possesses quite as many thorns as any briar. I'm only reporting what the song says.

To yours truly, a doubter if ever there was one, the tale told by the ballad seemed too good to be true. In the interest of truth, therefore, I undertook to visit Scarlet Town, many leagues from London though it is, and investigate the story. There I learned that Barb'ry Allen, far from being a thorny corpse, is very much alive and residing a couple of towns away. When I promised her that I would tell the world what really happened, she agreed to grant me an interview.

First let it be said that the years have been unkind to Barb'ry Allen. After Sweet William perished, she married a blacksmith with more muscle between his ears than in his arms. She lives in a filthy hovel with three or four scabby children scratching in the muddy dooryard along with the chickens. Her looks would no longer turn a young man's head. Crueler still has been the impact of the ballad, which, she says, drove her from her home into a town full of strangers who all know that the ballad is about her. But let her tell the tale.

Q: Who was Sweet William?

ALLEN: Sweet, my arse. William was an overweight, pimply-faced, self-centered poser. Why, he actually stalked me for months after I refused to marry him. He hung around the well when he knew I'd be filling my bucket there. Did he ever offer to carry my bucket for me? Of course not. He didn't want to get calluses on his soft white hands. He followed me to the market every Wednesday. He thought I didn't see him. Hah! The pudgy creep was so clumsy that once he tripped over a bushel basket of apples at the fruit-vendor's stall and fell flat on his face, apples rolling everywhere. Everyone in town got a good laugh over that one, especially me. I heard later that he never paid a shilling for all the apples he bruised. Who would want to marry a man like that? Besides, why would I want to wed a dolt like William when Jamie the blacksmith, the strongest, most handsome man in the shire had already asked for my hand? When my parents consented to let me wed him, I was overjoyed.

Q: Then what happened?

ALLEN: When the marriage banns were read, William just got worse. He found a worn-out old lute somewhere, probably in Lord Morton's trash heap. He and his mother lived on the manor, you see. She laundered Lord Morton's smallclothes. That was her job. Anyway, most of the strings were broken, but that never bothered William. He couldn't play a tune on any number of strings. He fancied himself quite the singer, though. He dragged that old lute out one summer night and stood under my window to serenade me. Well, you never heard such caterwauling. Speaking of cats, even the toms in

Scarlet Town were embarrassed for William. The neighbors, God be thanked, chased him away. They pitched overaged eggs and rotting cucumbers at him until he was covered with slime. When the pub closed, one of the drunks dragged him off to the millpond to clean him up. Somebody else trampled the lute into splinters.

Q: What put a stop to this behavior?

ALLEN: Well, you've heard the song. William gave up trying to win me by the usual means. He paid a visit to the herb woman who lives out in the woods and asked for a potion that would make me love him. Well, of course, she's a fake. She had no such thing. She gave him some concoction or other, though. William was so stupid he didn't understand that he was supposed to get me to drink the stuff. At least I guess that's what happened. He must have swallowed it himself.

Q: Why would he do that?

ALLEN: I have no idea. Maybe he expected it to transform him into a strapping young man, as handsome as my Jamie. But it made him sick. He went home and died, whining to his mother that he died of a broken heart. My fault, his mother claimed.

Q: And the town believed this?

ALLEN: Somebody must have. You know the ballad.

Q: What about the graves in the churchyard? The rose and the briar?

ALLEN: Well, they buried William there. In hallowed ground, even though some said he meant to kill himself. After all, he told his mother that he was dying for love.

The rose? And the briar? Go see for yourself. William's grave is there, all right, and it's covered with dandelions. As for my grave, I'm not ready for it–not with four brats all squalling for their porridge and me with another one on the way. My Jamie's a real man, all right, and he makes sure I know it, every night, without fail.

Q: Then who wrote that ballad?

ALLEN: William's mother made it all up to punish me.

Q: Did it?

ALLEN: Sure it did. My parents couldn't hold their heads up, not when everyone began singing that song right in their faces. Da found Ma hanging from the rafters one day, and then Da drank himself to death. Jamie and I had to leave town and set up shop over here. Even here, people snicker when they see me. I know they're saying — "There's that hard-hearted bitch who killed poor Sweet William." If they only knew. I slave in this cottage all day, and my Jamie sweats all day in the forge. Some days I'd like to toss him in the river when he comes home, stinking of old sweat and moldy leather, wanting to bed me.

Q: Do you ever wish you'd just married Sweet William?

ALLEN: What do you think?

Q: I think I'm ready to interview Lord Randall's sweetheart — the one who they say fed him poisoned eels.

ALLEN: Who says? The unfortunate Lord's mother?

Q: However did you guess?

And so, gentle readers, forget Sweet William and Barb'ry Allen. Forget the rose and the briar. Throw away your printed broadsides. Minstrels, now that you know the truth, you must tune your harps to a new song. The folk will forgive you.

Fish Story

Lyonell of Lyonesse, an ambitious young man aspiring to knighthood, cantered his horse through the enchanted wood surrounding the great Lord Caradoc's castle. Only yesterday an aged hermit who'd shared his meager stew with Lyonell had warned the youth about the perils of the wood. "It belongs to the Good People, the fairies," the hermit had said, "and they don't take kindly to trespassers."

But the road to the castle was long and winding, and Lyonell's horse was old and weary. The path through the wood showed clear before him and seemed much more direct. Lyonell was not a superstitious young man. Secure in his youthful strength, he decided to ignore the hermit's warning, never considering that possibility that the old man might possess the wisdom of many years' experience.

Aside from the swaybacked old nag he rode, Lyonell quite looked the part of a would-be knight. He wore colorful raiment that only a noble youth could afford. His hair shone golden under a plumed white cap. His scarlet tunic was belted with gilded leather gleaming with gems. The gems were really just glass, but they looked impressive. His cobalt blue riding breeches matched his eyes. Silver spurs adorned tall boots of black cordovan. On his right hand, hidden by soft kid gloves, Lyonell wore his one real treasure—a ring of purest gold set with a carved sapphire.

As soon as Lyonell entered the wood, he left the bright day behind. The gnarled trees grew so closely together that their boughs blocked the sun's rays. If Lyonell had been less intent on hurrying to his destination and more observant, he might have seen eyes peering down at him through the leaves— many pairs of eyes, set in faces not quite human. He might also have realized that the road subtly shifted as he progressed, steering him well of course.

Riding is thirsty work, and the young man was grateful when he entered a glade deep in the wood and discovered a spring bubbling up through the twisted roots of an ancient oak tree. He dismounted and led his horse to the water, for a knight should always see to the care of his steed before he indulges his own needs. But no matter how hard Lyonell tugged at the reins, the old gelding refused to approach the spring.

Lyonell shrugged. "Have it your way, then." He clambered over the oak's roots to satisfy his own thirst. But the only way he could reach the water was to lay prone across those roots and sip directly from the spring.

Aaah! The sparkling sweet water tasted even better than fine French champagne, he thought, though he'd never had the good fortune to encounter champagne. Lips to the water again, Lyonell attempted to take another sip.

The water rose up, curling around Lyonell's head and shoulders like tentacles. Strong though he was, he could not resist the monstrous pull, which dragged him headfirst into the spring. He struggled to swim free, but the malevolent water carried him down until he could no longer hold his breath. He gasped for air, knowing that this act would force water into his lungs but unable to help himself. He would drown. Lyonell had time for a moment's regret — he should have taken the road after all.

Wait! Lyonell sucked the water into his mouth, and it flowed out through his gills! He would not die in a watery grave — he was breathing. But he was no longer a young man. He was a fish, swimming in a stream whose bottom was lined with sparking stones. Tempted by their colors, he tasted some and accidentally swallowed one as he darted among the reeds and grasses lining the banks. Well, no harm done.

Then Lyonell was interrupted in his course by a net closely woven of silver threads. He was caught. Though the threads looked thin, his desperate thrashing could not break them, and he was lifted out of the water by a group of laughing maidens.

As Lyonell lay on the grassy bank, flopping in the net, he heard the ladies talking, admiring the lustrous scales that banded his sides. "What a lovely necklace his ruby scales would make," said one. "See how they catch the light."

"I'd have the cobalt scales," said another. "I'd sew them onto the hem of my dress, so that when I dance in the moonlight, I would be a whirl of blue brilliance."

"The topaz for me," said a third, "to adorn my raven-black tresses on Midsummer Eve."

Lyonell, the poor fish, realized that if the ladies wanted his scales, they'd have to scrape them off his body. And that would hurt. He thrashed more vigorously, trying to break free of the net, but to no avail.

The ladies placed their catch in a creel lined with cool, wet moss. They closed the lid over him, and when next Lyonell saw the light, it was to see a kitchen boy armed with a serrated fish scaler. As the ladies watched, making sure they would get their fair share of the lovely fish scales, the lad grasped Lyonell by the tail and began to scrape at the fish's side.

Lyonell discovered he had a voice. He gurgled a watery plea, "Please don't hurt me! I'll give you what you want!" And he began screaming in the kitchen boy's grasp, and—a wonder!—the scales dropped off of their own accord, in orderly rows of color, until there was nothing left of the Lyonell's fishy raiment, and he was clothed only in his slippery gray skin.

Each of the fairy ladies — for fairies they were — scooped up scales in her chosen color and placed them in crystal cups. Then they turned to leave.

"Wait!" said the kitchen boy. "You owe me payment for my work!"

"What do you want?" asked the maidens.

"I want this fine fish for my dinner," replied the kitchen boy.

"Very well," said the maidens. "You may have the fish."

The kitchen boy took up his filleting knife. He tested the edge of the knife with his thumb and placed Lyonell on his finny back.

The fish was now crying, "Please save me! Somebody please save me!" But the kitchen boy paid no attention. He applied the knife's sharp edge to the fish's belly.

All the maidens had gone off except one.

"But here we have a talking fish," said she. "This is no ordinary creature. Surely we can't kill a talking fish. Tell me, fish, what will you give to save yourself?"

Poor Lyonell was now gasping, for even a magic fish in the land of Faerie can't breathe air. He coughed a watery cough and lo! he spat out the bit of gravel from the streambed, and it turned out to be a lovely golden pearl.

The fairy maiden took the pearl between her thumb and forefinger. "Here, kitchen boy, take this pearl in payment for your work. It will buy you a fine fish dinner. I will keep the talking fish."

The maiden returned Lyonell to the mossy creel. She carried the creel and its prisoner back to the flowing spring, where she sank the creel into the water. The fish gratefully sucked water through its gills while she considered her prize catch.

Removing creel and fish from the water, she addressed her prisoner. "Fish, I have none of your scales, nor any pearl from you. What will you give me if I let you go?"

Lyonell whimpered, "I have nothing left but my flesh," and a tear welled up in his cold and staring eye. "I don't want to die. I just want to go home."

Her interest aroused, she asked, "Where might your home be?"

He replied, "Down the stream, where this spring's waters well up among the roots of the old oak tree."

"Alas for thee, poor mortal, you can never return there, for you have drunk the sweet liquor of the magic fountain of Faerie," she said.

"But there I was a man, and here I am only a naked fish."

"If you have something of worth to give me, perhaps I could free you from your piscine state."

"Only release me into the magic waters once more, and I will bring you my own golden ring, set with a carved sapphire as blue as the waters of this fountain. But I must go back to the spot where the waters pulled me in, for that is where it fell from my hand."

The maiden considered. The spot where the waters welled up into the mortal world was close by. But could she be sure the fish would return? Perhaps it would find its way to the deep pool where the salmon who knew all the secrets of the world dwelt. Who could guess what might happen then? So she took a silver cord and strung it through the gills and mouth of her captive, so that he could swim but not flee.

"Bring it back to me then," she ordered, "and we shall see."

Lyonell dove deep with a flip of his tail and made his way back to the spot where the old oak's roots drew sustenance from the water. There, where he had entered the stream, lay the ring that had once graced his mortal hand. Grasping it between his fishy lips, he bore it back to the maiden and spat it onto the bank.

Taking it up, the fairy held the ring to the light and then placed it on her finger, admiring the depths of the carven sapphire and the sheen of its golden setting. Then she felt the tug of the cord on her finger and looked down into the waters where her captive fish awaited. The magic waters had given him a full new set of colorful scales, and he looked quite handsome.

"My, how lovely you've become, my little treasure," said she. "It's back to the kitchen with you, so I can have all of your beautiful new scales."

"Oh, no, you don't," replied Lyonell in a much deeper, firmer voice. He flipped out of the water onto the grass, spitting out the cord that had leashed him to her. "One drink of the magic spring turns a man into a fish. A second drink turns the fish back into the man."

Lyonell stood naked before her, tall, muscular and handsome, with golden hair and blue eyes and red lips. He seized the fairy maiden and laid her down upon her back, parting her stockinged legs and taking her on the spot. She squirmed and wriggled just as he had when he was trapped in her net, but he had no mercy on her. "If I'm forever trapped in this world, I intend to enjoy its pleasures," and with that he plunged into her.

"Very tasty, that," Lyonell said, rising and smiling when he was done. Satisfied, he threw the lady into the stream, where the magic waters transform selfish fairy maidens into crayfish. She scuttled backward under a rock, antennae waving in fear.

Lyonell turned his gaze away from the water and toward the flowery meadows and towering castles of the fairy realm. Somewhere in those castles, he knew, he'd surely find other fairy maidens to ravish. Smiling, he placed his sapphire ring upon his finger and strode off jauntily in search of Faerie's most lovely ladies.

Sign of the Black Horse

In the little town of Steadby-by-the-Stream, on a Midsummer's Day, young Davey Darden inherited the old Crown Pub from his father. A willing worker, Davey refurbished the establishment and then settled down to await the arrival of the itinerant artist Pomfret Pounce, for it was known that without one of Pomfret's hand-painted signboards, no pub in West Shire would thrive.

Pomfret always knew when he was needed, and in his own good time, his colorfully painted wagon, pulled by a sturdy gray pony, stopped in front of Davey's pub. Brandishing a fistful of brushes, Pomfret clambered down from the wagon just as tavern-keeper Davey emerged from the pub to greet his guest. "Well, what'll you have?" said Pomfret to Davey.

"A sign, a sign," replied the hopeful Davey. Pointing to the drinking establishment he commanded, the tavernkeeper said, "This 'ere's now the Black Horse Pub, and 'e needs a signboard."

"Oh, aye, I know what's needed," acknowledged Pomfret, baring a smile full of gold teeth as he strode into the pub. Sitting down at Davey's well-polished bar, he said, "Travelin' around the countryside is thirsty business. Bring me a tankard of your toasty golden ale, not too much foam, mind you, and then we'll talk."

Davey filled two pewter tankards, one for Pomfret and one for himself, and prepared to listen, for no one told Pomfret what to do. The sign painter raised the tankard to his mouth and smacked his lips. "It's glad I am to see that you know good ale as well as your old Dad did," Pomfret said. "Now here's what I'll need to make your new sign. First find a piece of well-aged oak and have it cut into the shape of a warrior's shield — "

"Tis ready for you," said Davey, who knew what was expected of him. "And what will your artistry cost me?"

"Well," said Pomfret, "all I'll ask for the job is five gold guineas and as many mugs of your best ale as I need to finish the job. A slice of your roast venison now and then would go down nicely too. Give me that, and I'll paint ye your black horse, rearin' up so fine, with a rider in a silver doublet, a crimson cloak and a black cap with a white plume. When I'm done, people will come from the villages all around to admire your new sign, and once they've ogled it, they'll recognize that yours is the finest drinking establishment in West Shire, and they'll stay to eat and drink."

Davey the tavernkeeper sighed. He could manage the five gold guineas, barely. The ale was another matter. Pomfret Pounce was both a prodigious drinker and a painstaking painter. He would take his time about the job. Pom would down at least a barrel of ale—never mind how much venison—before the signboard was properly finished. But though Pomfret's price was steep, his work would be worth it, for all innkeepers knew that people would go out of their way to see the sign painter's work and spend their silver at the Sign of the Black Horse.

Many days later, when the signboard was complete and hung to Pomfret Pounce's satisfaction, the painter finished off the last mug of ale in the barrel and accepted his guineas plus a generous tip. Satisfied, he packed up his brushes and his paints, shook the innkeeper's hand and climbed back onto his wagon, clucking to his gray pony. The last Davey Darden saw of Pomfret Pounce, the painter was headed down the road toward East Shire, the wheels of his wagon raising a cloud of dust behind him.

Meanwhile, in the village of Raggles-on-the-Moor, Tamsin Townsend waited anxiously for Pomfret Pounce to make his appearance. Tamsin had owned the White Lady tavern for many a year, but lately business had fallen off, thanks to an upstart publican in the next village. She knew that only a Pomfret Pounce signboard could save her.

When at last the itinerant artist arrived, Tamsin begged, "Paint me a signboard with Lady Godiva on her milk-white steed." Not a wealthy woman, Tamsin shivered when Pomfret Pounce named his price for the new sign — five gold guineas and a barrel of East Shire's best ale. But Tamsin agreed to his terms, for she knew the results would be worth every penny. So Pomfret painted the beautiful maiden Godiva perched sidesaddle on a high-stepping white palfrey, holding reins strung with silver bells. Godiva's long yellow hair, entwined with a garland of red roses, scantily veiled her best assets, leaving little to the imagination.

While he worked at the Sign of the White Lady, Pomfret drank a few more quarts of ale than just a barrel and ate pounds of Tamsin's spicy pork sausages before he finished, but when he had done, Tamsin was happy, for news of her signboard spread rapidly through East Shire, and her clientele soon surpassed that of her upstart competitor.

Back in Steadby-by-the-Stream, all went well at the Sign of the Black Horse until the full moon, when merry revelers stumbled out of the pub at closing time and discovered that the black horse and its rider had vanished from the sign. There remained only a white silhouette where the colorfully painted image had been. Davey the tavernkeeper was appalled and a bit frightened but kept his own counsel until the next morning. Then, in full daylight, it could be seen that the horse and rider were back in their accustomed place. It was just a trick of the moon and maybe too much drink that had fooled last night's guests, thought Davey, and he went inside to wash down the bar.

That same night, miles away in East Shire, a party of well-sauced apprentices emerged from the

Sign of the White Lady precisely at midnight and looked up to admire Godiva's golden hair and buxom figure. But the painted maiden and her horse had vanished, leaving behind a black silhouette on the golden background. Tamsin the tavernkeeper panicked and drank so much of her own ale that she passed out on the floor of her establishment. But the next morning, Lady Godiva and her prancing mare were back in their accustomed place on the pub's signboard. Tamsin allowed herself to believe that too much drink had set her imagination to working overtime. Despite a ferocious hangover, she concluded that all was well.

And so it went, month after month. At midnight when the moon was full, the black horse and its crimson-cloaked rider and the yellow-haired lady and her white steed vanished from their signboards, to reappear a few hours later when the sun rose.

News of these strange phenomena spread throughout the land, and every month, when the time of the full moon neared, the merely curious joined the seriously thirsty outside the Black Horse and White Lady taverns, hoping to glimpse the miraculous events. They were not disappointed. At midnight in West Shire — you could set your watch by it, if you had one — the black stallion–for the horse's gender had become evident the morning after its first disappearance — and its noble rider vanished from the tavern sign. They stayed away until sunrise, when their image reappeared on the signboard outside the Black Horse as mysteriously as it had vanished. Likewise, in East Shire, the meticulously painted portrait of the fair-haired maiden and her milk-white mare faded from view, returning at the day's dawning. The tavernkeepers marveled at their good luck in convincing Pomfret Pounce to paint their signs, and they gleefully watched their fortunes grow.

For many a year, the man and the maiden and their steeds disappeared and reappeared with perfect predictability. But as the old folks liked to say, nothing is as constant as change, and so it proved. On a warm moonlit night in June, the images vanished, leaving their silhouettes behind just as they had always done. But they failed to return with the dawn. The tavernkeepers Davey and Tamsin and their clientele milled about for two days and nights, drinking and eating until they fell asleep on the floor or on the ground, whichever was closer. The fullness of the moon faded and the new lunar cycle began, and still there was no sign of the missing images.

In hindsight, the folk of East Shire, at least, should have seen it coming. Both mare and maiden had grown inexplicably rounder in recent days. And in West Shire, the black horse had gradually shifted his stance. No longer rearing, he placed all four feet on the ground and bore his rider, it seemed, with greater care.

A bit after nightfall about a week after the black horse and its rider had abandoned Davey Darden's tavern, the pub's patrons heard a tinkling like silver bells and the clatter of hooves on the cobblestones. The hoofbeats halted outside the tavern, and a very loud whinny sounded. The tavernkeeper flung open his doors, and his patrons surged out of the dimness to see what was causing the commotion.

On the following night, the scene was repeated at Tamsin Townsend's establishment: the thud of hoofbeats, the tinkling bells, and the high-pitched whinny, bringing Tamsin's patrons out into the chilly night to learn the cause of all that racket.

And this is the story that the grandchildren and great-grandchildren of the patrons of the Black Horse and the White Lady relate to this day: The images that Pomfret Pounce had painted were so very lifelike that whenever the moon became perfectly round, the black horse and its knightly rider became flesh and blood and galloped along the road to East Shire to court the golden-haired maiden and her high-stepping mare. One thing led to another, and in due time, a baby was born, and a foal. The noble couple came one last time to see their admirers, the maiden now wrapped in the knight's crimson cloak and cradling an infant in her arms, and the knight leading a black and white colt in a jeweled leather halter. They say the lady smiled, and the knight spoke the only words they ever heard him say. In a deep and even voice he told them, "It's now we must leave you, for our family has become too large for your cleverly painted signs."

Sometimes at the full of the moon, a tavern patron stumbling home after imbibing too much good ale reports that he has seen the man and woman, the black horse and the white, the baby and the colt riding toward the green hill where the fairies dance, and Pomfret Pounce opens the gate in the side of the hill so that the noble couple might enter.

As for the tavernkeepers, when next an itinerant artist visited and offered to repaint their signs, Davey Darden, owner of the erstwhile Black Horse, requested a signboard bearing only a crown, and Tamsin Townsend of the former White Lady wanted only a red rose. The painted crown, however, was fit to adorn the head of a king, and the rose was perfection beyond all nature. And when the moon is full, the tavern patrons are careful to down their last swallow of ale well before closing time, for who knows what they might see if they dare to look at the tavern signs at midnight?

hard travelin'

Amoebas at the start
Were not complex;
They tore themselves apart
And started sex.

— Arthur Guiterman

The Rolling Crones

"This looks like a good place to stop." Dorella Hart pointed toward the exit ramp.

Her comrade-in-vice, Minerva Biggs, was steering their big RV up from Sarasota along I-75. "Bushnell. Never heard of it."

Dorella waved the campground directory at Minerva. "This here book says there's lots of trailer parks in Bushnell. Near a VA cemetery too — should be plenty of American Legion posts around here."

"Veterans are always good for business," agreed Minerva. "Let's have a look."

"We need more estrogen cream — and soon." Dorella opened her purse. "We're short of cash.

"Maybe we can hit up a pharmacist in town for a free stash. If he's willing to take it out in trade — well, maybe we'll get lucky.

"You mean he'll get lucky. This is Florida, land of the old geezers. And we're the Rolling Crones, the hottest hookers to ever hit this burg. Don't you dare forget it!"

Dorella was 64 and Minerva was 62. Estrogen cream was vital to their business — which was serving up sex to old coots the young whores just laughed at. Estrace for themselves and Viagra for the johns. Fortunately they had a plentiful supply of the latter.

The first RV campground they came to was packed with expensive big rigs. Not the place for them — too many nosy neighbors who might not approve of the Crones' business enterprise. They kept on driving until they found a rundown trailer park where the Winnebagos and Dutchmen were green with decades of accumulated algae. The manager of the place was old enough to become a customer himself. With a wink and a leer, he directed them to a site ideal for their purposes — easy for customers to locate but far enough from the other residents to avoid any complaints about excessive nighttime traffic.

"Perfect," said Minerva once they'd set up the RV's drain hoses and got the electricity turned on. "This place is cheap — and private."

"Yeah, and that old bald-head at the front desk knows where all the retired Army vets hang out. Not only that, he says this town is jumping with biker gangs and Harleys. It's got so most of those Hogsters are older than we are."

"Don'cha just love those long white ponytails hanging out from under their helmets?" Minerva mimed a stroking motion "And how 'bout those soft white beards? I'll take a tickle from one of those any time."

Dorella grinned. "I always did like a little rough trade. Besides, bikers got plenty of money. They pay real good."

The Rolling Crones' RV had two queen-size beds, one at each end of their mobile whorehouse, curtained off for privacy. In the window over each bed hung red lights—heat lamps. When anybody asked about those lights, both women swore they were good for arthritic aches and pains. Their clients knew better, of course.

Before a week had passed, their old RV was rockin.' Word spread far and wide, to senior citizen centers, assisted living facilities and biker bars: "If you can't remember the last time you had a good roll in the hay, go visit the Rolling Crones!" The local pharmacist turned out to be one of their biggest fans, and he always brought plenty of Estrace and Viagra when he came calling.

Donny Ray Crisp, a retired Marine captain and the current leader of the Hog Eyes biker band, sent the Rolling Crones more clients than the parks' main road could handle. So the Crones got permission to hire a bush hogger to cut a side road into the park, straight to their RV. It worked. The residents quit complaining about the roar of the bikes. Most of 'em were half-deaf anyway. It wasn't cheap, but Minerva and Dorella wrote it off as just another cost of doing business. And it was a good business indeed until the day the law came calling.

"Jackpot!" announced Dorella one afternoon when Minerva was coming home with the groceries. "That fat old sheriff, Henry Ford Catrett, showed up with a warrant for our arrest."

"What's so good about that?" demanded Minerva.

"Listen up, girl." Dorella was almost purring. "I showed that old goat such a good time he tore up the warrant and gave me a nice tip besides. We've got the law on our side, and you know what that means."

Minerva raised both thumbs. "We've got it made in the shade. Nice work."

The next day the sheriff stopped in again. Good thing Minerva was home. When Dorella screamed for help, Minerva knew right away it meant big trouble. She burst into Dorella's curtained cubicle and found her partner in sex crime pinned underneath the obese sheriff. Dorella was gasping for breath. Henry Ford Catrett was clearly dead, gone to his maker at the height of his ecstasy.

Minerva pushed at the body and Dorella squirmed, but they couldn't roll heavy Henry off Dorella. Good thing Donny Ray was the next scheduled customer. That Marine might have been old, but he was still strong enough to rescue Dorella.

"Well," said Dorella once she could breathe again. "What are we going to do now? Never had anybody die on us before. And it would have to be the sheriff!"

"Anybody finds out what happened here, it won't be just the sheriff who's dead meat. They'll charge us with murder and have us in the pen in no time!" wailed Minerva. "What are we gonna do?"

"Calm down, sweethearts." Donny Ray's voice was soothing. "We'll wait until after dark and then dispose of the body in the swamps. I'll go get my SUV and we'll haul him off."

"You'd do that for us?" asked Dorella, who hadn't yet bothered to get dressed. She looked pretty good despite stretch marks and cellulite.

"Sure, as long as you'll give me what I like for free."

Minerva got out a mirror and applied a liberal smear of lipstick to her wrinkled lips. "Guess we can do that," she agreed.

Donny Ray showed up at midnight with his black Explorer and a biker buddy. The men dragged the sheriff's stiff body out of the RV and forced it into the back of the SUV, tossing a ratty old blanket over it.

"Okay, girls, get in the back seat," said Donny Ray. "We're going to take this good ol' boy to the Green Swamp and feed 'im to the gators. Won't be any evidence left—I guarantee it."

"This is creepy," moaned Minerva, "drivin' around with a dead body like this."

"Won't be much longer," Donny Ray assured her. "Good thing the moon's out. Easy to see where we got to go." The ex-Marine pulled off the highway onto a rutted dirt road. After about half an hour, he came to a boat landing, where he stopped the vehicle. "Everybody out now," he ordered.

The sheriff's body went into deep water with a reassuring splash. More splashes in the vicinity of the corpse assured the Rolling Crones and their escorts that the gators were doing their job.

Rubbing his hands together, Donny Ray said, "That's it, everyone. All done. Gals, let's go back to your place and have us a nice celebration."

A spotlight flared, focusing on Donny Ray's SUV. Three men jumped out, guns aimed at the old hookers and the white-haired bikers. "Federal officers! Hands up!"

"Wha?" said Donny Ray. "What've we done? What's going on?"

"Feeding alligators is a federal offense," said one of the officers.

"No shit?" sneered Donny Ray. "Never knew that. Guess there's a first time for everything."

Dorella winked at Minerva. "Don't worry about a thing, dearie. These lawmen are just old farts who aren't getting any pussy from their dried-up wives. Just you wait—we'll have 'em in our beds before they know what hit 'em. We'll never go to jail."

"Guess we'll just have to work a little harder for our Estrace," said Minerva.

"Hey, what about me and my buddy?" objected Donny Ray.

"You'd better hope at least one of these geezers like boys," smiled Dorella. "Either way, I guess you could say you're screwed."

"Like hell," said Donny Ray. "Nobody messes with a Marine no matter how old he gets."

The feds had arranged themselves in a line halfway down the boat ramp. Donny Ray and his buddy dived at the men. Donny Ray tackled two at once and his buddy got the other. The feds fell into the water. Trouble was, Donny Ray and his pal went with them. The water roiled with gators lashing their tails. Splash! Snap! Snap!

"I guess we're finished here," said Minerva, climbing behind the Explorer's wheel. "Good thing Donny Ray left his keys in the ignition. Let's go, Dorella. It's time we headed for greener pastures. The Rolling Crones are about to hit the road again. I hear there's plenty of horny old geezers in Arizona."

If you liked this book, would you please take a couple of moments to write a review on Amazon.com? Every review is important!

Any suggestions or corrections can be addressed to me at jillsvobodawriter@gmail.com. I'd like to hear from you.

And remember, these stories are works of fiction, and the people and places described in them emerged strictly from my imagination!

About the author
Jill Vogel Svoboda

Jill Svoboda has enjoyed a long career as a writer and editor in Chicago as well as a professor of literature at Northeastern Illinois University. Her fiction first appeared in a Chicago-based magazine, *A Great Read*, which published her novella, "The Lily and the Rose." She has won awards for her fiction in various writers' competitions, including the annual Writer's Digest writing competitions. Most recently, Svoboda received the Rosebud Magazine Mary Wollstonecraft Shelly Award for Imaginative Fiction.

She is passionately fascinated by things seen and things not seen, by what might be and what might have been, and her stories reflect this fascination. She is currently at work on a sword-and-sorcery fantasy series titled *The Powers of Surt*. The first book in the series, *Hostages to Fate*, will be published in 2017.

Svoboda resides next to the mysterious Withlacoochee State Forest in north central Florida together with her husband, Al Svoboda, who is a poet and a sculptor.